the Dreamway

Lisa Papademetriou

HARPER

An Imprint of HarperCollins*Publishers*

First Edition

This book is dedicated to Mary Yun and Dalila Gomes. They know why.

In a Wonderland they lie,
Dreaming as the days go by,
Dreaming as the summers die;

Ever drifting down the stream—
Lingering in the golden gleam—
Life, what is it but a dream?

—FROM "A BOAT BENEATH A SUNNY SKY" BY LEWIS CARROLL

THE BIRD

ETHEL B. STRINGWOOD MIDDLE SCHOOL was too drab for daydreams. The building was a squat rectangle with walls the color of depressed oatmeal. The teachers never declared that "learning is fun!" or told their students to "reach for the stars!" They did their jobs just as the building did—they offered the basics and didn't much care if you enjoyed yourself or not.

Stella Clay respected the building's honesty. Her twin brother, Cole, didn't agree.

Still, Stella *liked* the color of the walls and the old-sweater smell of the hallways. She appreciated the dingy film of dust that covered the windows. Stringwood wasn't trying to be liked. It was just doing its job.

It was stable, dependable. *Besides*, Stella often

thought, *the fun of a drab place is that when something wonderful happens, it's such a surprise.*

That was what she was thinking, in fact, as she stared through the window of room 106B. There was a tree outside the window, a lovely ginkgo with beautiful, golden fan-shaped leaves in the late summer and disgusting, squashy, cheesy-feet smelling seeds in the fall. At this moment, it was spring, and the tiny leaves were a pale golden green. And on one of the highest branches perched Stella's friend, a blue jay. *Monsieur Bleu*, as she thought of him (for room 106B was a French class). He wore the blue tuft of feathers on his head like a punk rocker and the markings around his beak gave him a permanent cheeky grin. He was building a nest right beyond the window, and Stella would occasionally catch his eye, bright as a bead of oil.

Stella liked to watch Bleu fuss over his work. It reminded her of the way her father would tug at the bedcovers to get them just so in the morning, smoothing away every imaginary wrinkle and bit of lint. Her mother always let the bed stay unmade. She said it didn't make sense to straighten it out if you were just going to mess it right back up at night. Her father, on the other hand, said that making the bed gave your whole day a good start. Stella thought that both of her parents made good points, but she could see that Bleu would side with her father.

The bird placed a slender twig just so, then turned to look at Stella. He cocked his head as if to say, *Well, what do you think?* Stella nodded in an encouraging way, but he turned his back to her and adjusted the twig.

She wasn't offended that he clearly didn't think much of her taste. After all, she had very little experience with nests.

"Mademoiselle Clay," her teacher said, "would you care to conjugate *rendre* for the class?"

Stella snapped to attention. Madame French (how horrible, Stella thought, to be a French teacher with the last name French) smiled that sneering little smile that teachers must learn in Teaching School—the one that says, *I know you were not paying attention and now you will suffer.* Stella sighed. Madame French was young and good looking, with long braids that she wore loosely piled on top of her head. She blinked a long, slow, *I'm waiting* blink. "We are looking for the *nous* form."

"I—uh—" Stella looked at the smartboard, but it gave no clues.

Connor Molloy snickered. He turned around in his seat, so that she could get the full impact of his smirk. Connor had thick brown hair and freckles and a round koala-looking face. On this particular day, he wore a hat with little green army men glued to the top. (It was School Spirit Week at Stringwood, which was supposed to reflect devotion to the school and its values. Those values, apparently, included a deep-seated respect for crazy hats and a day devoted to wearing them.) Connor looked like a nice guy, maybe a guy with a good sense of humor, which just proved that looks could be deceiving.

"Mademoiselle Clay?" Madame French repeated.

"I . . . don't . . ." Stella looked over at her best friend, Renee Semedo, who shouted, *"Nous rendons!"*

Madame French turned to her with sternly arched

eyebrows. "Renee," she snapped, "I thought we had discussed this."

"I couldn't stand the suspense!" Renee cried, and half the class giggled.

"Please, try to control yourself," the teacher told her.

Renee pushed her purple-framed glasses back up onto the bridge of her nose. "I *do* try," she replied. "It just doesn't work."

Madame French put a hand over her eyes, shook her head, took a deep breath, and turned back to Stella, who cringed in her seat.

"Now, Stella—" she continued. "Please give us the *elle* form—"

Thunk.

Stella caught the flutter out of the corner of her eye as Bleu dropped to the ground.

"It flew into the glass!" Connor shouted as Stella bolted out of her chair.

"Everyone, return to your seats!" Madame French cried, attempting in vain to be heard amid the bustle of scraping chairs and running feet as the class moved toward the windows. *"Retour à vos sièges!* Stella Clay! Get back here!"

But Stella was already in the hall, lurching awkwardly toward the double doors. She burst into the cold spring wind, which prickled her face as she raced toward the gingko tree. The branches grew close to the window, and Bleu lay near the roots, not moving. He rested on his side, his claws curled into tiny, gnarled fists. For a moment, Stella too was frozen, afraid to touch him.

He was her bird, though. Hers because she had watched him and cared about him and felt that she knew him, so she moved forward. Cupping her stiff right hand, she gently scooped him into her palm with the other. He was still, but his heart fluttered against her skin. She kneeled there, feeling his quick, steady heartbeat, ignoring the cold at her nostrils, her fingers. Madame French thudded a fist against the window, and Stella looked up into the furious face of her teacher. *"Rentré ici!"* Madame French's voice was muffled behind the glass, but her expression was fierce enough to melt steel.

One windowpane over, Renee pressed both palms against the glass, her eyes fixed on Stella's hands. For crazy hat day, Renee wore a headband with golden ball-shaped head-boppers. They bounced at the end of a long metal spiral all around her halo of brown curly hair. Renee nodded in a way that meant, *go ahead*, and the boppers wobbled encouragingly.

Stella wasn't sure what to do with Bleu. She only knew she couldn't just leave him. Shivering, it occurred to her that the bird might be cold, so she brought her hands closer to her mouth and blew warm air over him. He didn't move, so she repeated the motion, her breath warming her own palms cupped protectively around the bird.

Bleu jerked suddenly and hopped to his feet. His scratchy, twiggy little claws pricked at her palm for just a moment as he cocked his head and looked at her accusingly, then—in a thrum of feathers—fluttered away, disappearing around the corner of the drab gray brick.

Stella wiped her hands on her jeans and stood up. She looked up at the window, and she heard Madame French's muffled voice as she shouted in *en Français*. The faces began to disappear from the window, but Renee lingered a moment and gave Stella their secret signal: an index finger curved into a hook that meant, *I'm with you*. Shivering, Stella signaled back and then headed across the dead grass patched here and there with ice, back toward the iron-gray double doors.

★

By the time Stella returned to room 106B, the class was once again reciting past-tense conjugations. They looked at her with nervous eyes, but no one spoke a word or even paused in the conjugation. Only Connor narrowed his eyes and crinkled his nose. Madame French did not look in her direction when she entered the room. Her hand shot out, holding a small slip of paper. Stella plucked it from her fingers. A detention. Renee winced at her sympathetically.

With a shrug, Stella headed for her seat and slid into her chair. She'd never gotten a detention before. She was a bit surprised at the ordinariness of the paper. It wasn't fancy or anything. It wasn't even on special colored paper, like the kind they used for flyers.

Well, what did you expect? she asked herself. *A golden ticket?*

Sighing, she tucked the slip into her homework notebook and glanced out the window. Bleu still hadn't returned to his branch, but it didn't matter. He had flown away. He was all right.

And that meant he would be back.

Stella had faith.

★

"That was amazing," Renee gushed as she and Stella joined the crowd tramping toward the cafeteria. "I thought that bird was dead, and then you were all, like, Bird Whisperer! What did he *feel* like in your hand?" Behind her glasses, her huge eyes managed to add as much commentary as her actual mouth.

"Light," Stella replied. "Soft. His feet were . . . skritchy."

Renee waited for more. When it didn't come, she said, "You should be a poet."

"Cole's the one who's good with words, not me."

"He's also the one who's good with hats," Renee remarked, eyeing Stella's pink knit cap.

"This was the craziest thing I could find," Stella insisted. "It's Mom's."

"How is that hat even crazy?"

"I never wear pink," Stella pointed out.

"Oh, hey, look—the STs are doing another food drive." Renee paused in front of a table decorated with a blue Students Together tablecloth. Two large cardboard boxes sat on top, half full of jars. The banner at the front of the table read "PB&J—Bring It!" in vibrant, graffiti-style letters.

"Peanut butter and jelly? That seems weirdly specific. Do I like this idea? I don't know." Renee often narrated her thoughts aloud as she was having them, which Stella usually found funny.

Besides, Renee spoke her mind. Literally and figuratively. Stella liked that. She never had to ask herself a question like, *Is Renee mad at me?* because Renee would tell her right away. Renee turned to Alice Yun, who sat behind the STs table, smiling. "Do I like the idea of a peanut butter and jelly drive?" Renee asked her as classmates streamed through the doors to the cafeteria behind them.

"You don't just like it. You *love* it," Alice Yun replied from her place behind the table. Her "hat" was made of paper, with a small green cone at the top attached to long yellow flower petals that stuck out around her head. "Peanut butter and jelly are two of the most requested items at the food bank. They last a long time, don't have to be refrigerated, and make a quick, no-cook, nutritious meal packed with protein. Here's some more info," she added. She handed over a card and smiled, revealing a dimple in her right cheek.

"Wow—I *do* love this idea!" Renee replied, scanning the card. "You were so totally right!"

"And you can bring soynut or sunflower seed butter too. Because some people are allergic to peanuts," Alice went on. "We'll be collecting jars all week."

Renee turned to Stella. "We're so doing this!" She looked past Stella and shouted, "Hey! Phoebe Marshall! Bring in some peanut butter!" A girl wearing a popcorn bag stuffed with cotton balls on her head gave a thumbs-up before being swept along in an eddy of seventh graders.

"Who made the sign?" Stella asked, eyeing the banner's graffiti style. "It's really cool."

"I did," Alice replied, smiling shyly. "My dad helped me bring it in."

"Well, *we* are bringing in foodstuffs," Renee told her. "You can count on us!"

"Glad to hear it," Alice said. She waved to a couple of eighth graders in squid hats who quickly made their way to the front of the table as Renee and Stella stepped away.

"She is so cool," Renee whispered to Stella, "with her homemade hat and her amazing sign."

Stella nodded. Alice was something of a Stringwood celebrity; everyone knew who she was. Stella had seen people staring at Alice's wheelchair, but she had never heard of anyone asking her about the accident. Sure, plenty of people claimed to know the Official Story, but Stella had heard everything from "her father was a drunk driver," to "she was hit by a car the day before

Christmas," to "she was on a bicycle without a helmet." That last one made the least amount of sense, as there was nothing wrong with Alice's head, but that didn't stop people from repeating it.

Stella and Renee made their way to their usual table along the left-side wall. The cafeteria was also the auditorium and the recess space on rainy days, and it always smelled like a strange combination of limp broccoli, commercial cleanser, and armpits. Ramlah was already there, sitting with Katie and Other Katie. All three wore hats shaped like goldfish, with open mouths that looked as if they were swallowing the girls' heads. Other Katie smiled and gestured to the seat beside her, which Renee slid into.

"You guys *have to* bring peanut butter and jelly tomorrow," Renee announced.

"Okay," Ramlah said, and Katie agreed. "Def." Everyone knew that it was useless to argue with Renee.

A boy with bright, dark eyes turned in his seat at the table behind theirs. Stella's twin, Cole. He wore a hat made of tinfoil with a tiny green paper alien taped to the top. "Some crazy rumors going around today,"

13

he said, taking a bite of mini carrot.

"Stella got a detention!" Renee announced.

"Oh, you've heard about it." Cole grinned. "But I knew it couldn't be true."

"It is, though," Stella said with a wry grin. "Will you wait for me?"

"What's a brother for? You've waited for me often enough." Cole got detention at least once a month because he hardly ever paid attention in class. He was usually too busy drawing or writing in his notebook.

It was a problem, that notebook, because Cole insisted that he should be allowed to write in it whenever he wanted. It was his Work, as he called it, after all. He was *Working*. That's what you do in school.

Stella pulled out a small container of carrots and a cheese sandwich—the twin lunch of her twin's lunch. She took a bite of sandwich to hide her grateful smile. She and Cole were different, but she knew that he was thinking the same thing she was: neither one of them much liked going home alone.

It was then that Connor walked over to Stella's table. Two other guys in baseball hats with plastic army men glued to the brim stood behind him. Matt and Jason looked like they were trying hard to copy Connor's confident swagger and angelic expression, but it was coming off as backup thuggery.

Freakishly tall for middle school students, Stella thought, watching their approach.

"Hey, Turbo," Connor said to Stella. "Nice jog to save your bird." He clamped a stiff right arm against his waist and stumbled several steps in imitation of Stella's awkward run. His clones laughed.

"Shut it, Connor," Renee snapped. Her golden head-boppers quivered indignantly.

"Nice coordination, Connor," Cole teased, "no wonder the basketball team is in last place."

"Cole," Stella warned, but she didn't really know how to finish the sentence. She didn't enjoy being made fun of for her rigid arm and leg, but neither did she like the look in Connor's eye, which was something like a flash of lightning before thunder rattles the ground. Connor's lips twitched as he sized up Cole.

"At least my dad can come and cheer for me at games," Connor snarled.

"Ohmygod, are you a complete *idiot*?" Renee stood up and actually chucked a strawberry fruit gummy at him. "Shut up!"

Ramlah and Other Katie chimed in. "What's wrong with you?"

"That's just rude!"

"Why would you *say* that?"

"Get out of here, Connor," Renee warned him. She used her low and dangerous voice—the one that made people listen.

"I was finished, anyway. Come on, guys." Connor flipped Cole's tinfoil hat from his head and stalked off. Jason sneered as Cole stooped to retrieve his bent, ruined hat. Matt shot a last glare at Stella before following Connor to the other side of the cafeteria.

Stella took a sip of water, to try to swallow the lump that was rising in her throat. She didn't understand why Connor disliked her so much. She had never done anything to him; at least, nothing that she could remember. He didn't seem to like Cole, either, but it was harder to tease him and he was better at standing up for himself.

Stella could never think of anything to say until

days or even weeks after she had been made fun of. Only then would the perfect insult appear, much too late and almost always in the shower, where it was perfectly useless.

Cole crumpled his tinfoil hat into a ball and then stood up to throw it into the garbage. At the table, his friends Emmett and Zeke had already moved on and were discussing some video game and the many ways that one could blow up a zombie.

Renee plopped back into her seat. Then she reached out a crooked finger and linked it around Stella's right pinky, as she had been doing since they were four and one of the kids in preschool—Kasey—had said that she didn't want to play with Stella because of her "weird arm." Stella couldn't squeeze back very hard, but she wiggled her whole hand. For once, Renee didn't say anything. She just held on and didn't let go while the rest of the lunchroom carried on, eating, oblivious to the fact that Stella's heart had been ripped from her chest and stomped on, and though he might not look it, Cole's had too.

THE DARKNESS MOVES

"How was it?" Cole asked as they made their way down the street. The clouds had blown through, leaving a clear sky in the fading afternoon light. The block's mixture of old and new trees stood sentinel, and most seemed undecided as to what season they were actually in. Two were nearly in full leaf, while several were still bare, but most sported leaf buds and seemed to have an optimistic attitude despite the chill air.

"Detention was surprisingly boring. I just sat there reading," Stella confessed. "I had expected, like, heavy lifting or scraping the gum off the underside of the desks."

"It depends on who you get," Cole explained. "Ms. Nunez makes people clean. Mr. Samuelson doesn't make anyone do anything—he just sits and reads the paper. You can even get up and walk around. It's practically a party when he's in charge."

"I had Ms. Khan."

"Oh, yeah. She likes to use that time for planning, so she lets everyone do homework."

"It's kind of sad that you're such an expert," Stella told him.

"It's not so terrible." Cole shrugged. His glance darted toward the right, then flicked straight ahead. "He's there. Don't look."

She looked, of course. He was in his usual place, standing by the stoop, as if he couldn't decide whether or not to go back inside. His steel-gray gaze followed them as they walked. Cole edged a little closer to Stella.

"What are you starin' at?" the man growled.

Cole and Stella had learned from experience not to respond to this question.

"Keep on movin'. Don't give me that look. Everybody's always lookin' at me." The man's gaze followed them like the eyes in a haunted painting. The face never moved, but the rage flashed from beneath a tangled mass of gray hair. The hem of his olive-green pants was frayed and ragged, and his navy hooded sweatshirt was caked with filth.

The kids at school who walked this way called him Angry Pete. Nobody knew how they knew his first name, they just did.

Angry Pete looked at Cole. "They'll get you," he snarled. "Better watch out."

Stella walked as quickly as she could manage as the man continued to speak not *to* them, but *at* them. Cole stayed close to her side.

Angry Pete was always there. He lived in the basement apartment, and he spent his time fussing with the flowers that grew in the little patch of garden right in front of his place. It was a potted Eden that bloomed at any time of year, but Stella and Cole feared him in spite of the flowers. He was scary—Pete and his furious eyes.

It was why they didn't like to go home alone.

The entrance to the subway line was a stairway that led directly into the ground. Stella liked the way she would be walking on the sidewalk and then suddenly disappear down the stairs into the earth. But, today, Cole paused at the top step.

"What?" Stella asked.

"He said something—in like a whisper."

"What was it?"

"They'll get you," he replied. There was something in Cole's eyes, a dark movement, like a ripple or a wave. She had seen it earlier, when Connor said that thing about their dad. "Why did he say that? Why say it to me and not you?"

"What do you think he meant?" Stella asked. She had no idea.

"Some kind of . . . creatures from the Underworld, maybe." Cole was eyeing the steps at the subway stop.

"Those steps don't lead to the Underworld," Stella told him. "At least, they never have before."

"Yeah," Cole said. "But you can kind of imagine it, can't you?"

"Nope," she replied. "I'm not the one with the great imagination." Stella moved toward the stairs, and by the time she was halfway down, Cole followed her.

"I'm terrible at imagining creepy stuff."

"Like a skeleton with a snake coming out of the eyehole?" Cole suggested.

"Sorry. My brain is incapable of picturing it."

"Really? What about a zombie rat with acid blood?" Cole took the stairs in twos: *thunk*, *thunk*, pause. *Thunk*, *thunk*, pause. Zombie-like. "Or a flesh-eating watermelon?"

"That's not even a thing!" Stella laughed.

"I know. That's the point!" With a grin, Cole paused on the steps and folded his arms across his chest. "Come on, try and think of something scary. Anything!"

Stella shifted her backpack higher onto her shoulder. "A black cat?" she said after a moment.

"What?" Cole burst out laughing. "Stella, we *have* a black cat!"

"And she's scary!"

"No she isn't."

"She *can* be. When she's in a bad mood, and she's all—" Stella batted the air with her left hand.

"Lola is about as scary as a jelly doughnut," Cole replied.

Stella tried to keep a straight face. "*Jelly* can be terrifying. When you think about it."

Cole grinned. "Wow, you are really bad at this."

"I know! But I'm good at other stuff."

"Says who?" Cole teased.

"Dad. You can ask him," Stella suggested.

"I will!" Cole crowed. "I can't wait to tell him that you've developed a sudden jelly phobia." His voice turned soft. "I hope he calls soon."

"He'll call sometime tomorrow," Stella said. "He has to." She pulled out her card and slid it through the slot in the silver turnstile. It beeped and allowed her through. Cole did the same and they headed to the right.

It was an odd time—4:10—and the station was nearly empty. This wasn't uncommon; Stella and her brother didn't live in the center of the city, where there would have been a press and crush of bodies at any time of the day or night, but on the outer edge of it. They headed toward where the front of the train would be once it arrived. *Prewalking*, Cole called it. Stella stared down past the end of the platform into the tunnel in the direction the train would be coming. Sometimes you could see the light from as far away as the stop before theirs. But Cole turned and faced the darkness in the other direction, the darkness that was directly in front of them and much closer.

Stella turned toward him. "What are you looking at?"

"Just—nothing." He laughed a little. Then he pulled his backpack around the front of his body and unzipped it. After digging around for a moment, he pulled out his notebook.

The problem with having a good imagination is that you could really use it to torture yourself. Cole had a brilliant imagination, and he mostly used it to write poems and create stories about Lyrrin, a fantastical country that he had made up in his head. His notebook was full of pieces of poetry, myths and maps, characters and creatures. Not all of Cole's stories were pleasant. In fact, many were gruesome in a thrilling sort of way. Sometimes, those stories affected Cole's mood for days. Their friends knew Cole as someone who was charming and funny, but Stella knew he was like the ocean—what you see on the surface is blue sky and sparkling water, but there were also depths, dark and vast and full of dangerous things.

"See that?" Cole asked.

"What?"

"There's something there. Can't you kind of . . . see it?" Cole asked. "Like, if you look into the darkness enough, you can watch it . . . move."

Stella looked down the tunnel. She saw the usual blackness of pipes and electrical wires and filth.

"You can imagine how it reaches down and, maybe, there's a river. Like the Styx. And a whole city of the dead. Or maybe a forest . . ."

Stella looked into the darkness. Her imagination was not like Cole's. It was good, but mostly for figuring out how to fix things or how to take them apart. Still, she could almost see what he meant. When you looked into the darkness, you saw whatever your imagination supplied. Like—

She sucked in her breath.

Cole looked up from the page. "What?"

"Nothing, just—"

But he saw it, too, and it startled him so badly that he dropped his notebook. It tumbled and fluttered, trailing pages, until it flopped onto the silver rails. Cole stared at it for a moment. Then he looked in the direction that the train would come from. It was still clear.

"Don't you dare—" Stella told him, but Cole had already jumped down onto the tracks. This wasn't the first time he had done it, although he knew it was dangerous. Last year, Stella had dropped her house key from the platform, and Cole had jumped down to retrieve it. She had appreciated it but had been furious with him too. He could have been killed!

He picked up the notebook and straightened. Then he looked back into the darkness that had moved.

A black drop wept from the ceiling, splashing silently into an oily puddle on the filthy tracks. The silver rails stretched into darkness in either direction. Overhead, fluorescent lights flickered their eerie, yellowish glow, making the few people on the subway platform look like they were just getting over a case of intestinal flu. The pungent stink of urine crawled up Stella's nostrils and settled there as if it intended to stay. The subway oozed and dripped, thawing from the frigid winter, leaving a thin scum of filth over everything that dared to venture below the crust of the city.

"Cole?"

Cole looked over at her then. He had to tilt his head up to look at her, and when he did, he looked worried. "I think it's a dog." Then he turned back toward the dark. Even when the subway is quiet, the silence is pierced with the buzz of electricity, the clangs and creaks of movement in the depths of the shadowy tunnels. "Is it?" Cole hissed under his breath. He tucked the notebook under his arm and started toward the darkness. His eyes were like pools again, vacant, almost as if he didn't realize he was moving.

"Cole? What are you doing?" Stella shouted. "You'll get run over. You'll get electrocuted!" She followed his gaze and caught a movement. The shape was odd—it was the size of a large dog, but the head was the wrong shape and the rear legs moved with an awkward, lurching gait that didn't seem . . . friendly.

"Just a sec," Cole called over his shoulder.

"Hey! You're not supposed to be down there!"

shouted a woman in a velour tracksuit, but Cole ignored her. He trotted toward the far end of the platform and disappeared into the shadows of the tunnel.

Nervously, Stella turned in the opposite direction. There was nothing but blackness, the void of empty space. And then, suddenly, a glimmer. The tiniest spark. It was the light of a train. It was still at least a full stop away. Ten blocks. "Cole," Stella screeched. "Train!"

"It's still far away—I'll be right back," Cole promised, then tripped down the track shouting. "Hey! Here, boy! You've got to get out of there!"

Stella looked at the businessman beside her. The man kept his eyes glued to his newspaper, pretending not to hear.

"Don't go near it!" Stella shouted, but Cole didn't hesitate or turn back.

Stella tried to quiet her fears. She told herself that Cole was helping, that the dog's owner would be grateful, but when she imagined the shape, she shuddered.

She turned to look at the train. She could see the white light, small as a firefly, but growing. "Hurry," she whispered. "Hurry." She didn't dare go after him.

How would that help? She'd never be able to get back onto the platform, not with her stiff leg and arm.

Cole wore a navy sweater and jeans. As he loped down the tracks and into the darkness, all Stella could see clearly was the white collar of his shirt. The rest of him melted into shadow.

She turned again. The headlight was larger now. She could hear the rumble of the metal wheels against the tracks. "Cole!" she called.

Her brother cried out; his white collar dropped to the tracks. "Cole—no! Help!" Stella turned to look for someone—anyone—to help her, but the business-man was shouting and the woman in the tracksuit was screaming and neither of them were going to be any help at all. And now the train was at the other end, roaring into the station with a fury so large it swallowed her in sound.

Hot air blasted Stella in the face, making her hair stream behind her. "Help!" she screamed again, then turned to the tracks. Now her hair whipped into her face and she dipped her left foot over the platform edge, about to jump. Just then, Cole appeared—his face smudged, his expression blank.

Brakes screamed and so did Stella. "Cole! Cole!" she shrieked, and her brother was as still as a statue. "Cole!" she screamed again. "Move! MOVE!"

He staggered toward her, and she knelt on the platform's edge. Reaching for him with her left hand, she yanked him by the collar. Her right arm flailed stiffly but caught nothing; there was no way to brace herself. "Help me! I can't lift you!" Her face was a fraction of an inch from his, and she looked into his eyes. They were black—the pupils huge—but she whispered his name, and something flickered in them, like a small star at the center of a black hole. His eyes snapped to the train.

"Now!" Stella cried. She gave a final, furious haul as Cole pulled and scrambled one leg up, over the edge of the platform. He fell forward and they rolled, arms and legs linked as they had been in their mother's belly, away from the edge as the train finally came to a stop with a hiss just two feet away.

The train driver, fat and furious, stuck his head out of the driver's booth, unleashing a storm of curses. But Cole and Stella clambered to their feet and melted into the stream of people that swirled and eddied from the doors of the subway cars. They did not speak as they walked through the length of the carriage and exited at the far end, crossing between cars and entering the next. They did not speak as the train started up and they walked through another door, then another. They still did not speak as they slid onto the bench, a space for each of them, beside each other.

They did not speak for three stops. Stella felt as if her stomach had been scooped out, like the guts of a pumpkin, and set to the side. Beyond the window that faced them, the walls of the subway tunnels—dark pipes and twisting wires—slipped by. She saw Cole's face in the shadowy reflection. He was pale. But not a normal state of pale. He was pale in a ghostly way, as if he were a reflection of a reflection. She turned to look at her brother to make sure that he was still there and solid.

Cole must have felt her looking at him, because he said, "Don't tell Mom," just as the train turned, with a sudden lurch and screech of the brakes, to bury itself deeper into the tunnel.

"I won't," Stella replied. She was fairly certain that she never wanted to talk or think about what had just happened ever again. "Or Dad."

Cole turned to her then. "Yeah," he said.

"Where's your notebook?"

"I—I left it."

"You left it?" Stella felt a pain in her chest, like a throbbing bruise. "Oh, Cole!"

He shrugged, and Stella was surprised at how unconcerned he seemed. "What choice did I have?" he asked. Then he *flickered*.

There was no other word for it—like a film strip or an imperfect hologram, he flickered. He disappeared for a half second, then reappeared. Stella felt the blood move in her heart slowly, thickly. She had the strangest thought that he wasn't real. She reached for his arm and touched the edge of his sleeve before he moved his arm away.

His sleeve, at least, was solid.

"What happened to the dog?" Stella asked.

Cole looked at her in the face then. "It wasn't a dog."

"Then what—"

"It was enormous. It scratched me and ran away." He held out his arm and pulled back his sleeve, but there were no scratch marks. Cole's eyebrows knit together in confusion. "I *thought* he scratched me."

"It's good he didn't or you'd have to get a rabies shot."

Cole flexed his arm. "It doesn't hurt anymore."

"That's good," Stella said.

Cole, white faced and stony eyed, nodded. "Yes," he agreed.

But Stella wasn't sure it was good. She wasn't sure what any of it meant. And she wanted to feel sorry for the dog—or whatever it was—that had run away and disappeared onto the tracks, but mostly she just felt frightened that it was still out there. Somewhere.

THE EYES IN THE CLOSET

WHEN STELLA AND COLE GOT home, they were greeted by a smile in human form. "Look who's finally here!" Aunt Gertie called, letting out a hooting laugh. "Come into the kitchen and say hello to your father!"

"Dad's up?" Stella asked, but Cole just blinked. When they stepped into the bright kitchen, they saw their mother leaning toward a laptop. She was sitting beside Renee, who was telling the story of Stella saving the blue jay, which was much more dramatic than the version Stella remembered.

"Here they are!" Gertie announced. "James, I have given Stella a long lecture about the value of staying in class," she said to the handsome man on the screen. Gertie wasn't really their aunt; she was their mother's oldest friend and Renee's mom. People are often said to have a twinkle in their eye, but Aunt Gertie was more like a one big twinkle all over—she shone and giggled and swirled like a running brook and, like a brook, was a refreshing sight to behold.

"The troublemaker's home!" James said. He flashed a smile that reached out from the computer screen like a hug and cocked his head in a way that reminded her of Bleu.

"Dad—I know I shouldn't have run out of class—" Stella glanced at her mother, who frowned and shook her head.

"Finally sent to the principal's office!" her father went on. "I'm so proud!"

"I was *not* sent to the principal's office," Stella replied.

"Jim—" her mother began.

"Oh, Tam—of course my little chickadee is going to help a bird." Jim winked, and Stella felt an ache in the center of her chest. Her father liked to tease; Stella never got into trouble. She was a practical girl, and trouble didn't seem worth the effort. But she missed her dad and the way he managed to encourage both her (who got into trouble too little) and Cole (who got into trouble too much).

"How's it going over there?" Stella asked. "Did you get the grid sorted out?"

Jim nodded. "We managed to restore power to about half the area," he said. "People are so relieved—it's been out for months. Did you get the photos I sent? Me and the transformers?"

"They're bigger than I thought they would be," Stella said. "They always look small in the diagrams."

"They have to be a good size to get that much power." Her dad grinned.

"What time is it there?" Stella asked.

"It's about one fifteen in the morning," her dad replied. "Late. But I wanted to be the first to say happy birthday to your mom!"

"We still have until tomorrow," Stella pointed out.

"But here, it *is* tomorrow. I didn't want to get into trouble." James put a hand up to the side of his mouth and pretended to whisper, "You know how she is." He rolled his eyes dramatically.

Tamara smiled. "I get such a bad rap."

"Where's Cole?" James asked, and Cole, who had been pouring crackers into a bowl, turned from the counter to wave at the computer.

"Oh, yeah, Dad, Cole wanted to ask you . . ." Stella's voice trailed off. "Dad?"

James continued to smile from the screen, but he didn't move. "Oh, he's frozen," Renee said. She traced a light finger across the touch pad. "Can you hear us?"

The picture on the screen flickered, and Stella felt the tiny hairs all over her body tremble. She felt Cole standing behind her chair, and she remembered how *he* had flickered, just for that one moment. . . .

Words reached out to them in choppy blurts. "Jim, we can barely hear you," Tamara announced into the computer.

And then—suddenly—his head shifted to the right, and the picture was back. "How's this? Can you hear me now?"

"Yes," the room chorused.

"Hey, Cole wanted to ask you something," Stella said, scooting over to make room on her chair for Cole, who sat beside her.

"Yeah, I—" her brother began.

"Just a second, Cole." Jim looked over his shoulder and nodded at someone they couldn't see. "Yeah," he said, then turned back to the camera. "I may have to go in a minute—"

"No problem!" Aunt Gertie chirped from the stove, where she was stirring something that smelled of spices and heat. "We want to eat!"

"Are you saving some for me?" Jim asked.

"No! We are eating your share," Aunt Gertie sing-songed in her lilting accent.

"Okay, well, hey, Cole, I—" The words were cut off.

"He's frozen again," Renee said.

Tamara took the computer back. She clicked and double-clicked. "Ugh!" Then she hung up the call and tried again. There was no answer. Sighing, she said, "Well, you know how the signal is there."

"The electricity goes out all the time," Stella agreed. "Sorry you didn't get to talk to him." She smiled gently at her brother. "Or tell him about my newfound fear of jelly doughnuts."

Cole shrugged. "Next time," he said vaguely. He nibbled another cracker.

Stella sighed, feeling a bit guilty for hogging screen time with their father. Cole had barely even had a chance to say hi to their dad, who might not get to call again for another couple of days.

"All right, who is ready to eat?" Aunt Gertie asked.

"Mom brought a cake from that new bakery!" Renee announced.

"Renee!" Gertie hooted. "That was supposed to be a surprise! Tamara, don't look in that box there. There's nothing for you to see! That's not for your birthday!"

Renee looked embarrassed, but Tamara laughed and gave her best friend a hug. Everyone knew that Renee was terrible at keeping secrets. To be fair, this was a genetic trait: Gertie was also lousy at it. They never gossiped—they just got so excited about things that they forgot when they were secret.

Stella looked over at her brother. He shoved a cracker into his mouth and crunched. He chewed and chewed as he stared near the computer screen. Not quite at it. More like over it, at the wall beyond.

"Cole! You stop eating those crackers," Gertie ordered. "I made a pot of *cachupa* rice, here."

"And I made the salad," Renee added.

"Why don't you wash your hands and go set the table?" Tamara took the bowl from his hands. "And Stella, you can get the water pitchers and glasses."

"Come on, Cole." Stella poked her brother in the arm. It took him a moment to nod and follow. It was almost as if he were receiving the signal from far away. From across the planet, maybe. Or from another galaxy.

★

After dinner, Cole said he had a headache, but Gertie wasn't having it. She insisted that he help clear the table before he lurched off to his room to be alone. Stella tried to catch his eye, but he really did seem to be feeling unwell. Between that terrifying moment on the subway and losing his notebook, it didn't seem that surprising.

He'll probably feel better in the morning, she told

herself. That's what people always tell themselves, and it is quite often true.

Stella's English teacher insisted that they read at least twenty minutes from an unassigned book every night, but she had just finished a nonfiction story about the race to build the atomic bomb and hadn't yet chosen a new one. So, once Gertie and Renee gave their hugs and goodbyes—and Renee reminded Stella to dig out an unopened jar of peanut butter from the cupboard for the food drive—Stella found herself rooting around the living room shelf, looking for something to read.

Most of the books were things she had read before or had no intention of ever reading, but a volume of classic fairy tales was laid across the top edge of several tomes, sticking out slightly. This was the kind of thing that Cole often read to inspire the mythology of Lyrrin. They weren't the cleaned-up Disney Princess versions—they were the originals, with people who were forced to dance themselves to death in hot iron shoes and whatnot. People in old-fashioned fairy tales had a lot of anger issues.

This wasn't the type of thing that Stella usually liked, but today—perhaps because Cole had lost his notebook or perhaps because she had to read something and nothing else struck her—she picked it up. She flipped through the pages and came to a beautiful illustration of Hansel and Gretel in front of a house made of gingerbread. It was a story that had always bothered her. After all, the parents had barely enough to eat. That was why they led the children into the woods and left them there. It was awful, but maybe it made a selfish sort of sense. Who could bear to watch their children starve? It was all pretty complicated when you really stopped to think about it.

She snapped shut the book with a soft thump and brought it to her room. Cole's bedroom was beside hers and his door was shut. No light leaked out beneath the door. That's good, she thought. He's asleep. Her heart gave a little flutter at the thought of the secret she was keeping from her mother. But what would be the point of telling her parents about what had happened on the train? They would just worry and punish Cole. Besides, he wasn't likely to do anything like that ever again. He didn't need punishment. He needed rest.

Stella brushed her teeth and changed into her favorite pajamas and then tucked herself into bed to read. Her mother was back at the kitchen table, working on her computer, answering macroeconomics questions. She was studying for a master's degree, and nothing—not even a birthday—kept her from her homework.

Stella found, to her surprise, that she enjoyed reading the familiar fairy tales. They felt easy on her mind, like a well-worn path through the woods. They lifted the heavy feeling in her stomach, the stone of not telling her mother what had happened in the subway. It was also fun to read an illustrated book. Stella had reached an age where most of the books she read were text only, which was fine in the way that her dreary school building was fine. She did not *object*, and even found some comfort in it.

But neither did she object to the illustrations. They were beautiful, and the lovely details—the tiny red mushrooms with white polka dots tucked halfway beneath a fern in the corner of the forest, for example—captured her imagination, making it easy to slip away to another place.

At nine o'clock, Stella's mother appeared in the doorway. Stella closed her book and folded her legs under the comforter as her mother came to sit near her feet. She pulled a purple marker from the cup on the desk and handed it to Stella. They both looked over at the calendar on the wall, and neither said a word as Stella marked through the white square that indicated the date with a slash. There were fourteen white squares left in the month.

"Soon," her mother said, but Stella was thinking about fairy land and how time stretched and changed there. What was the difference between fourteen days and eternity? They were both in the future—you couldn't touch either one. Neither one of them was *now*.

"Why do you think the Skype cut out?" Stella asked.

Her mother touched Stella's hair gently. "You know why. It happens. He'll call when he can."

"What if something bad happened?"

"Nothing bad happened."

"How do you know?"

"I know."

"But *how* do you know?"

Her mother leaned her head back against the wall. She closed her eyes for a moment. "If something bad happens, they'll call us," she said, "or they'll send someone over," and then Stella regretted asking. Her mother was right—the military always contacted the families first. She turned to Stella. "I'm supposed to say something to you about getting a detention."

"That really won't happen again," Stella promised. "It was just that this bird is—"

"Honestly, Stella, it's fine," her mother said. "I understand why the teacher was angry, but—you broke a rule, you got punished, end of story. If it happens again, we'll really talk. I just wanted to feel that I had done my motherly duty by mentioning—it—" Her voice cut off into a yawn.

Stella nodded.

Lola, Stella's long-haired black cat, came strutting

in and flopped onto the rug in the center of the room with her paws in the air.

"I swear that cat is part dog," Mom said, stooping to pet Lola on the belly. Clearly insulted, Lola grabbed at her with her paws and playfully bit at her hand. Then she rolled over, stood up, and stared at Stella's closet, swishing her bushy tail.

"Crazy cat."

"You hurt her feelings," Stella said.

"I can't worry about a cat's feelings," her mother replied. "She'll live." Bending over, she gave Stella a warm kiss on the forehead.

Her mother stretched out beside her and let out a yawn. Stella turned out the light on her bedside table. Her room was never entirely dark. Stella would have preferred darkness, but in the city, light leaked through the curtains, casting strange shadows in her room. In total darkness, there were no shadows.

Even in the dim light, Lola continued to stare at the closet in the unnerving way that cats have. Stella tried to ignore it. She snuggled closer to her mother, who was breathing deeply and evenly. There wasn't much point in waking her up to tell her to go to sleep.

The moment Stella shut her eyes, she heard it—a scratching sound from the closet. Her eyes snapped open.

A sweaty chill raced from Stella's scalp to her toes, but she didn't get out of bed. She told herself that she had imagined it. But the steady swish of Lola's tail said otherwise. The cat turned her yellow eyes to Stella.

Stella pressed more closely against her mother. The noise did not happen again. Lola walked to the closet door and tried to stick her paw underneath it. Eventually, she gave up on whatever she had imagined was there and hopped onto Stella's bed. Lazily, she turned in a circle—once, twice—and then lay down into a tidy Cat Donut.

The room was quiet except for the sound of her mother's breathing. There was a warm body at Stella's side and one atop her toes. She should have dropped off instantly. But although she was tired, her mind was busy clicking and buzzing with thoughts about Cole, and the subway train, and her father. After a reasonable amount of time of counting sheep (she pictured them in a herd, grazing quietly) she decided to open a window. She slipped her feet into a pair of flip-flops, clicked on her bedside lamp, and let in some air. Then she settled back on top of her covers with her book of fairy tales.

The temperamental spring weather had dried out and served up a warm evening. Someone was playing music, and a sad, unfamiliar guitar strain slipped in through the small opening between the sash and the sill. Outside, beyond the glass, the moon shimmered like an opal. Stella had read that, in the seventeenth century, an Italian astronomer named Riccioli had mapped the oceans on the moon. You can see the pattern of the dark waters when you look up.

There is only one problem—there aren't any oceans on the moon. The "seas" are actually ancient lava beds. They're made of rock.

But Stella had always loved thinking about Riccioli and his imaginary oceans. Sometimes, she even thought she could see them churn and roil on the silver disk.

She looked down at the book of fairy tales. She had

been reading "The White Cat," which was a lot like "Beauty and the Beast." Except in "Beauty and the Beast," the heroine saves the prince with a kiss. In "The White Cat," she saves him by cutting off his head and tail and throwing them into the fire. Also, instead of singing and dancing candelabras and teacups, the servants were floating, disembodied arms.

A tree branch tapped, tapped, tapped against her window, and Stella shuddered a little, thinking of the drumming of delicate white fingers at the end of bodiless arms. She tried to peer through the glass, but the small puddle of light cast by her bedside lamp made it impossible to see out. Instead, she found herself blinking at her own reflection as the strange music chimed on.

Then a small thump came from beneath her bed, sending a shock of fear through her nerve endings. She had just convinced herself that she had imagined it when there was another *thunk*, and then a yelp. "Ouch!"

If there is one thing that is worse than the feeling that there might be something underneath the bed, it is the absolute certainty that *there is something underneath the bed.*

Something that can talk.

Very, very slowly, she leaned over the edge of her mattress. With her left hand, she reached down and pulled up the dust ruffle. Two tiny eyes gleamed at her and she swallowed a scream. The monster darted out from beneath the bed and Lola pounced at it.

"Lola!" Stella cried.

The cat had streaked toward the door. She shot an accusing glare back at Stella, who realized that Lola had something in her mouth. It was silvery gray.

"You'll choke," Stella said, striding toward the cat. Lola took a tentative sideways step. "Drop it!"

The cat deposited a small mouse at her feet. Then she tucked her tail around her paws and looked up at Stella, as if expecting congratulations.

Stella looked down at the mouse, which was perfectly still. A small pouch hung from a string around its neck, and the mouse seemed to have dropped something.... A scrap of paper. Picking it up, she realized—it was a piece torn from Cole's notebook, the one he had lost on the train that afternoon.

What kind of mouse steals a scrap from a notebook

and then follows its owner home? She looked at the creature more carefully. It was larger than a normal mouse, and his fur seemed to cast a luminous glow. It seemed unreal, but as she bent to touch it, it squeaked. It looked at her, blinking, then grabbed the paper and darted toward the wall.

"Hey! Give that back!"

Stella lunged after it as the mouse ran headlong into the plaster. Tripping forward, she had just managed to grab the mouse by the tail as she fell against the wall— and kept going right through it.

THE MIDDLE OF NOWHERE

THE DISTANCE SHE FELL WAS no more than the distance to the floor, but she could tell by her soft landing that this was not her carpet. She was facedown in something that felt like wood chips. Stella sat up and brushed herself off, but when she opened her eyes, the whiteness of the sky and the wavy black horizon blinded her. She put her hands over her eyes for a moment. Heat pulsed down against her scalp. Wincing, she tried to open her lids just a slit. The sky was white, the ground was black, and the brilliance clawed at her vision. She shut them again, heart thumping and clanging.

She tried again, more slowly, and with lots of blinking. After a few moments, things came into focus. The sky was a washed-out, pale blue, almost white at the edges. The ground around her was black, except for the small bit she was sitting on. That was a mound of wood-chips which seemed to serve a few very sad-looking mums placed here and there. It was a median. She was seated on a median in a vast, empty parking lot. Music floated on the still air. It was a blandly cheerful tune that Stella felt certain she had heard before over the speakers at her doctor's office, and it had a tinny quality, as if it were being played on a toy saxophone.

A line of large buildings built in faux-Spanish hacienda style hulked nearby. It was . . . a strip mall. Stella read the names of the stores: *Impulse, Harmless Fancy,* and one called *Momentary Fascinator.* The buildings were set back at the center, where there was a large fountain featuring a bulging-eyed fish sculpture spouting a column of water.

Beside the fountain was a double door, like the kind on an elevator, set beside a Metro sign and a down escalator. And there, not ten yards away, something small and silver scurried away from her. The mouse!

"Come back!" Stella shouted, racing after it.

"Eep!" It squeaked and doubled its speed. Its tiny

legs pumped furiously, sending it hopping across the cracked clay, but there was nowhere to hide. Stella was awkward and slow, but the creature's small legs were no match for the length of her stride. Stella caught it easily in her left hand. She held it up and looked at its face, which was almost comical, with its overly large eyes and very fine set of whiskers. He was a lovely color, sleek as a dolphin, and he wiggled in her hand, flashing her an indignant glare. "I'll bite you," he threatened.

"Don't you dare," Stella warned. "I saved your life!"

"Oh, so it's like that, is it?" The mouse twitched his whiskers and sniffed. "We're going to argue over who did what for whom?"

Stella paused and stared at the rodent in her hand.

"I am talking to you," she said. She brought the mouse closer to her face. "HOW AM I TALKING TO YOU?"

"Believe me," the mouse retorted, "I'd much rather you weren't. Now if you would simply unhand me—"

Stella turned in a full circle and stared again at her surroundings. "Where am I?" she whispered.

The mouse scoffed. "As if you didn't know."

"Hey!" Stella had to stop herself from giving him a good shake. "I don't know what this is or who you are or *how it is that you can talk.* But you were in *my* room. You have a piece of *my* brother's notebook. Explain!"

The mouse rolled his eyes and heaved a sigh.

"Start with where we are," Stella ordered.

"Put me down," the creature countered.

"Not until you tell me where we are."

"I should think it was fairly obvious," the mouse said, "that we are in the middle of Nowhere."

"Not helpful," Stella replied.

"But true, nonetheless," the mouse said. "See for yourself." And he twitched his whiskers in the direction behind her.

Stella turned and looked more carefully at the Metro sign by the tree. It was an ornate iron lamppost at the top of which perched a sign written in curly letters. *Dreamway*, it read in all capitals. And then, below, *Nowhere*, and the escalator that led down into the concrete. Stella looked more closely at the elevator doors on the other side of the sign. They weren't connected to anything. They were just . . . doors.

"Where—?"

"Can't you read?" the mouse asked sarcastically. "If you want to get from Nowhere to Anywhere, you have to go into the Dreamway. We're right on the edge."

The moment he said this, the elevator dinged and the doors slid open. Twenty people spilled out. Some were carrying shopping bags or random items. One man held a black cat. A woman wearing a large, colorful turban carried an oversize, heavy-looking book. One or two headed into the shops, but the rest walked the short way from the elevator toward the escalator down into the Dreamway. They did not glance at Stella or at one another, and nobody spoke.

"Who are they?" Stella asked.

"Sleepers," said the mouse.

"What?"

"They're asleep," the mouse explained. "In your world. Barely just asleep. They're heading into the Dreamway for the night. We're on the edge of the Penumbra, right between Here and There."

Stella stared at the tiny mouse in her hand, who was clearly doing his best to look dignified.

"What's the Penumbra?" Stella asked.

"Not too bright, are you?" the mouse answered. "The Penumbra is the world you come from. The Shadow World."

"I come from the real world."

The mouse cocked his head. "Oh, *do* you?" He looked bored.

Stella scanned the landscape in every direction. There was nothing. Nothing but the strip mall, a single gnarled tree, the elevator doors, and the escalator down into Dreamway. "So the Dreamway is where they—sleep?"

"No," the mouse snapped. "They *sleep* in the Penumbra. The Dreamway is where they *dream*."

"That's not how dreaming works."

"Well, you're the expert, of course." The mouse twitched his whiskers haughtily.

Stella shook her head, and it occurred to her that, perhaps, *she* was the one who was dreaming. She slapped herself in the face and was very disappointed when it hurt the appropriate amount. "How did I even get here?"

"A question for the philosophers," the mouse remarked. "But I think I pulled you through by my tail. Not," he added quickly, "intentionally."

The last of the Sleepers was on the escalator now. It looked as if the old woman was sinking into the concrete. As Stella peered around again, she began to feel dizzy. She didn't like this place. It wasn't . . . anything.

Why did I come here? she thought, and then remembered. "Why do you have a piece from my brother's notebook? What were you doing in *my room*?"

"I'm a Door Mouse," the mouse said importantly. "I travel between the Here and There."

"What about this piece from the notebook?"

"I . . . found it." The mouse's whiskers twitched shiftily.

"Where?" Stella demanded.

The mouse tried to look away from her, so she held him right up to her eyes. "Fine," he snapped. "I found it in the Dreamway, all right? It was just sitting on a platform, so I said to myself, 'What's this doing here?' And I realized it had come from the Penumbra. It shouldn't have ended up in the Dreamway. Nothing and no one travels between the worlds without the proper authorization. But it seems as if a lot of unauthorized things have been happening lately, and I wanted to investigate."

"So—how did it get in?"

"Well, I don't know for sure, but I think—well, it's possible it was a Chimerath."

Stella didn't know what a Chimerath was, but the word sent a shudder through her. "What"—her voice was suddenly dry and raspy—"is that?"

"A Chimerath is—it's a shadow creature. They live along the Nightmare Line. But they're always looking for a way into the Penumbra. They're attracted to the brightness, you see. People with—with the brightness inside of them—"

"What does that mean?"

"Well, you know. A certain creativity. A certain lightness of spirit. They look for someone who has that brightness, and then they wait. The Chimerath wait until some darkness comes, and then . . ."

"What kind of darkness?"

"Fear," the mouse replied. "Sadness. Those things

are like a crack for the Chimerath to get through."

Stella swallowed. She didn't want to ask the next question. "What do they want Cole for?"

The rodent shifted, uncomfortable. "Well, ehrm. Well, they eat the brightness, you see. Suck it out of people like a bowl of pasta al dente." He slurped noisily, and Stella shuddered.

"So—that . . . thing that tried to get Cole. . . ?"

"It didn't *try* to get him," the mouse told her. "It got him."

Stella wobbled, as if the ground had suddenly become a tar pit. "What?"

The mouse pointed to the piece of lined notebook paper. "There's your proof. He's probably on his way to the Nightmare Line right now."

"But—Cole is at home! He's asleep in his room!"

"Yes—so are those people," the mouse said, gesturing to a tall woman wandering around the strip mall. "Well—that one's *almost* asleep. But the point is that the Chimerath doesn't take your body. It takes your spirit—the *you*ness of you. Are you following?"

Stella nodded, mute.

"Your *you* energy is very powerful. And if you can trap that energy—"

"You can use it," Stella finished.

Stella thought about the vacant look in Cole's eyes, the way he had *flickered*. "So Cole is—"

"He's here and he's there. But the important part of him . . ."

". . . is here . . . somewhere." Stella tried to stay calm and focus all of her energy on sounding reasonable. "But nightmares end," she pointed out. "People wake up. People must be able to get out."

"Get out?" The mouse looked blank.

"Yes—I mean . . ."

"Oh . . ." The mouse nodded. "Yes. Right. That's if they come in as a Sleeper. A Chimerath pulled your brother through a door. That's the difference between *having* a nightmare and . . . um . . . let's say, *becoming* one? The longer he stays down here, the dimmer his light in your world will become. Eventually, it will go out."

"And he'll be—dead?"

"No. His spirit will be. Wait—there's a word for it

in your world. He'll be . . ." The mouse paused dramatically. "A zucchini."

"A zucchini?" Stella repeated. "You mean a squash?"

"What? No. That's not—" The mouse shook his head. "Blank stare?" he prompted. "Muttering? Musssst . . . eeeeeat. . . brainssss . . ."

"A *zombie*?" Stella cried.

"Yes! That's it—thank you! A zombie!" The mouse paused, then added, "Only he won't want to eat brains, of course. That's only in movies."

Stella felt every bit of her insides tremble. She remembered the strange look in Cole's eyes and the way he had flickered on the subway.

Then, suddenly, an image of Angry Pete popped into her mind. Could Cole turn into—that? A frigid icicle of fear traced down her back.

"How fast? How fast will it happen?"

"Oh—it could take years. Or days. You never really know."

"*Days?*" Terror squeezed her heart. "How will you stop it? What are you going to do?" she demanded.

"Me?" The mouse huffed. "I'm going to take this

paper to someone who can prove where it came from then file a report!"

Stella nodded. "And then what happens?"

"Someone will look into the situation!"

"And then?"

Cheerful, tinny music bleated over the silence that hung between them. The fish fountain burbled on, oblivious, as the mouse let out a squirmy cough. "Well . . ." he admitted, "eventually someone might write a strongly-worded letter."

"A *strongly-worded letter*?" Stella screeched. "*Eventually*? Someone has to get my brother out of here *now*!"

"Well—then you'd have to go into the Dreamway, and that's—"

"Fine," Stella said. She began to walk toward the escalator.

"—ridiculous. What? Wait! What do you think you're doing?" the mouse squeaked. "You can't just walk in there and find your brother. You don't know where you're going! You have no idea where he is!"

"That's why you're going to help me."

"Why should I?"

"Because I have you in my hand, and I'm not letting you go."

The mouse thought this over. "Huh," he said at last. "I see. Good point."

"*Can* you help me?"

"Of course I can help you! I am, after all"—and at this he lifted his long silver whiskers a bit—"a Door Mouse. If I can't help you, then I don't know who can."

She looked down at the mouse. "Great. So what's your name, anyway?"

The mouse looked surprised. "Yes!"

"What?"

"No one has ever guessed my name before."

"I'm sorry, it's—what?"

"Not What!" The mouse looked deeply offended. "Of course I'm not What. *He's* a ridiculous toad. I'm Anyway!"

"Oh, your *name* is Anyway?" Stella repeated.

"Of course." Anyway shook his head with clear disgust. "And I had just begun to think she wasn't completely hopeless," he grumbled to himself.

Stella shot another concerned glance toward the Dreamway. It looked like a normal subway entrance, with the exception of the fact that it was in a strip mall and seemed connected to an elevator to nowhere.

She hesitated. *Those other people have already gone down there,* she thought, trying to reassure herself, *those Sleepers.* "Are you sure that's the only way?"

"If you want to get *some*where, you have to get out of Nowhere," the mouse replied. "Duh."

Sometimes, crazy things sound reasonable. This, for Stella, was one of those times.

Just in case, though, she smacked herself across the face again. It still hurt. She sighed and wondered what to do with the mouse. He was grouchy and furious at being held against his will, but she was afraid that if she let him loose, he would run away. That would, of course, be a disaster as she had no idea where she was or where she needed to go. The Door Mouse eventually suggested that she keep him in the little pocket on her pajama top. That way, she could keep an eye on him, but he wouldn't be strangled by her "giant walrus fingers," as Anyway referred to them. (*Do walruses have fingers?* Stella wondered. *Or were her fingers themselves like walruses?*)

So she put him in her pocket, where he was an unexpectedly reassuring spot of warmth against her quickly-beating heart.

Anyway seemed quite pleased with this arrangement. He stood with his paws at the top lip of the pocket, very much like a lookout in the crow's nest of a ship. From there, he could direct Stella where to go.

Stella stood at the top of the escalator, watching the steps vanish into the darkness below. It was decrepit, with a brass railing and wooden steps that clattered and shook. Stella did not want to step onto it. "It looks very old," Stella said.

"Old? Hah! It's ancient," Anyway agreed, but he said it in a proud, rather affectionate way.

"How do I know it's safe?" she asked.

Anyway laughed again. "Wait—are you quite serious?" he wondered.

"Yes."

"How do you know it's *safe*?" He looked at her sharply and twirled his whiskers. Half to himself and

66

almost as an afterthought, he added, "What *is* safe, my dear?"

Stella took a couple of deep breaths, watching the stairs sink into the landscape. Her stomach felt cold and queasy, her legs heavy. But she forced herself to take a step, and then another, and then another until she had gotten onto the escalator, which rattled on, unconcerned, taking her down below the asphalt crust that she had been standing on moments before. Anyway hummed a few bars of "Turkey in the Straw" as the escalator went on, down, down, down into the semidarkness.

"Ready, ready!" Anyway shouted, and Stella realized that they must be coming to the end. Escalators often gave her trouble, and the dim light made her nervous. She was preparing to step off when Anyway cried, "Mind the gap!"

Gap? Caught off guard, Stella stumbled forward and tripped. With a cry, she twisted as she fell to avoid crushing Anyway and managed to catch herself—with her right hand.

She brought her right hand up to her face and made

a fist—a tight fist. Gracefully, she wriggled her fingers. Her right hand had never been *flexible*. She could move it, yes, enough to get dressed, but it wasn't easy. Her wrist curled toward her body, and her fingers were stiff. Her right leg, too, dragged slightly. People hardly noticed it—Stella hardly noticed it—until she had to run, or dance, or climb a rope. Stella sat up. She pointed the toes on her right foot, then flexed. "Wow," she whispered. She stood up, and gave a little jump, and another. Then a skip she had never been able to do before, and it took a couple of tries before she managed a lovely, even series of skip, skip, skips. She stopped suddenly and waggled her fingers in front of her face. It was mesmerizing, the way she could make them move up and down, up and down, in a wave.

Ahem! The paper-crinkly sound of someone very small clearing a very small throat cut through her concentration.

Only then did she remember to check her pocket.

"Thanks for your concern," Anyway said drily. "You'll be pleased to hear that I was not crushed beneath the weight of your falling body."

Stella was barely listening. "I had a stroke. I had a stroke when I was a baby, and my hand doesn't—"

"Things are different here."

She spread her fingers, then clenched her fist again. "I'm healed."

"No." Anyway shook his head. "No—you're just in the Dreamway. It's like you're an avalanche."

"An avalanche?"

"You know—something that represents you. Like a projection of you." Stella still looked blank. "Like in a video game."

"An avatar?"

"Yes, that's what I said, an avatar. It's a little like that. Except that you really *are* here. *And* you aren't."

For the first time, Stella looked up. She was sitting on the floor, and before her, at a bit of a distance, was a subway station. But it looked nothing like the subway station that she visited every afternoon on her way home from school. This was a beautiful old-fashioned train station, with enormous stone columns and echoey marble floors. Arched windows were perched along the top of the walls, like birds on a wire. It looked like the kind of thing that someone would see in London or Paris. Stella had never been to either of those places, but the cities evoked elegance and grandeur, and that was what this train station was like. Several arched tunnels led off along the sides of the walls. Stella imagined that this was where the tracks were. She skipped again, enjoying the feeling of movement. *It doesn't matter if it isn't real*, she thought. *It* feels *real. It feels realer than life. It feels . . . easy.* She had to stop herself from running.

"We have to go." Anyway perched on her knee, then crawled up her sleeve and back into her pocket.

Closer to them was a large chrome arch guarded by a gargoyle on either side. Beside each gargoyle was a silver mesh container, like a large basket, about the size of a pickup truck. At the top of the archway was a television monitor, on which a man with a bad toupee—the TV said his name was Dr. Peavey—droned something about paperwork. The arch was strange, made of metal and brutal in design—a direct contrast to the elegance of the station beyond. It didn't belong; it looked like something someone had added recently.

"We'll have to get past the turnies somehow," the mouse said darkly.

"Turnies?"

"Turnstile operators. We've got to get past, and right away!" He tugged at her pocket, until she was forced to move out of fear that he would rip her favorite pajamas.

"Okay," she said. It didn't look too hard. For one thing, it wasn't a turnstile—just a big arch. It was sleek and silver, backlit with a glow like the moon. It looked out of place in the old station, positioned between gargoyles, as if it had traveled there from the future while the station had traveled from the past. There were no "turnies" in sight. Stella shrugged and took a step forward.

A gargoyle leaped in front of her and let out a bone-rattling roar. Stella screamed and threw her arms over her face.

"I was thinking you might try something a bit sneakier," Anyway told her. He faced the gargoyle. "Now, really, is that necessary, Horace?"

Horace, who had a beak and pitted eyes, ducked his head sheepishly. "Well, it's on Dr. Peavey's orders, ahkay? I had to stop her, right, Martha?" he asked, turning to the other gargoyle, who nodded.

"Oh, yeah." Martha nodded. "For sure."

Horace looked delighted. "All Sleepers gotta hand over any and all baggage before proceedin' troo da turnstile, ahkay?" Horace explained, just as the television image of Dr. Peavey droned, "All Sleepers must hand over any and all baggage before proceeding through the turnstile." Horace jutted his chin and tucked his long stone tail around his paws. "As I was *sayin'*," he added importantly.

"Them's the rules," Martha explained.

"That's right, them's the rules!" Horace agreed.

"Zip it," Martha told him. "They get it."

Horace ducked his stony head.

"I don't have any baggage," Stella said.

"What's that in ya pocket?" Horace demanded, pointing.

"That's me, you nitwit!" Anyway shouted.

"Well, ya bein' carried around, baggage-like," Horace went on. "Am I right, Martha?"

The other gargoyle narrowed her eyes. "This will

have to be investigated—forms filed, and other things."

Horace looked as if he were about to chime in, but with a glare from Martha, he clamped his gray lips shut.

"We're not filing any paperwork," Anyway snarled.

"Excuse me, I really need to get out of here," Stella said.

"Whattaya tawkin' about?" Horace demanded. "What kind of a Sleeper are ya? This is suspicious, am I right, Martha? I'm right, aren't I? Tell me I'm right."

Martha lifted a stony eyebrow. "This is gonna be a ton of paperwork. I've already got a migraine just thinkin' about it."

"Look, this is official Door Mouse business," Anyway said importantly.

The gargoyles looked at each other. Then they broke into stone-shaking laughter. Martha's laugh was a demure little *hiss-sss-sss*, while Horace's was a honking *haw-haw-haw*. It was as if an avalanche had a snuffling cold.

Anyway tried to look dignified. "Look, she isn't even a Sleeper!"

To Stella's surprise, that stopped the laughter right

away. Horace straightened up and eyed her. "I said she was suspicious, am I right, Martha?"

"*Another* non-Sleeper," Martha said thoughtfully.

"What does that mean?" Anyway demanded, an edge in his voice.

"This is the second non-Sleeper we've had today! The other one came through with a creepy something-or-other. I couldn't see. He had a hood."

"The non-Sleeper," Stella asked. "Was he carrying a notebook?"

"Oh, yeah," Horace said. "Sure. Tried to keep the notebook with him, but I got it from him! I got it from him, didn't I, Martha?"

"I was very proud when you told me," Martha said, and Horace dipped his head, clearly pleased by her praise.

"Can I see it?" Stella asked.

"Of course," Martha said. "Show them, Horace."

Horace's stone eyebrows shot up. "Er, now?"

"Yes, now."

Sheepishly, Horace pulled a few crumpled pages from a stone pocket. Stella stared at the pages that he held out to her. She knew that awkward, backward-slanting scrawl. It was Cole's. "But where's the rest?"

"The rest?" Martha glared at Horace.

"Well, I got most of it," Horace simpered.

"There's unaccounted-for baggage inside the system?" Martha's voice was brittle.

Horace cowered. "Just a bit," he admitted. "Part of some."

Martha glared as if she was about to smash him to rubble.

"Look, you've got to let us through." Anyway pulled a scroll from his pouch and unrolled it.

It was a very tiny pouch and a very fat scroll. "How did that fit in there?" Stella asked.

Anyway rolled his eyes. "Everyone from the Penumbra wants to talk about 'space' and 'time' and 'smell.' *Well, that's all different here!*" He unrolled the scroll with a flourish. It was very long, and the words written on it were so tiny that Stella couldn't read them. They looked like a series of dashes and dots, like Morse code. "It reads right here, 'Sleepers must surrender baggage to the appropriate turnstile operators. No sleepers will be allowed to remain in possession of aforementioned baggage unless they have filled out the proper paperwork in octuplicate and filed it with the Office of Undersight. Failure to declare baggage will result in detention of the aforementioned Sleeper.'" With a smug glance above the scroll, Anyway went on, "No mention of *non-Sleepers, is there*? Therefore we are free to proceed!" The mouse rolled up the scroll again and placed it back in the pouch.

"Well, he does have a point, Martha," Horace said.

Martha glared at him. "Do you know how much paperwork this is going to require?" she demanded.

Stella looked at the gate. Her brother was in there somewhere with some*thing* that was headed for the Nightmare Line. "If you let us through, you won't have to fill out any paperwork," Stella said, trying to be helpful. "And if we take these pages, there won't be any paperwork for that, either. It'll be like we were never here. Like it was never here."

Martha was clearly thinking it over. "Never here?"

"Never here."

"But you were here," Horace pointed out. "You're here now!"

"Shut it," Martha told him. "We're gonna close our eyes, and when we open them . . . never here." She winked, then put her paws over her eyes. Horace followed suit. "Go ahead."

Stella felt something small poke her shoulder. It was Anyway, who hissed, "Just go!"

Stella stepped, at long last, through the archway. In her pocket, Anyway shook and trembled, and it took Stella a moment to realize he was laughing.

"What's funny?" Stella asked him.

"Oh, nothing," he said at last. "You're a quick thinker, that's all."

"I am?" Stella asked. She found this somewhat hard to believe. "I think I just said the obvious thing."

"I don't think it would have been obvious to most people," Anyway agreed. "Not around here, anyway."

Stella tried to walk lightly as she traversed the grand old station. Although Sleepers moved through the space, their eyes unblinking as they made their way to tunnels marked with track numbers, their feet were noiseless on the marble floor. Stella's feet, on the other hand, were making extra noise.

Flip-flop flip-flop flip-flop.

Besides the Sleepers, there were other people in the station. A bear in a gray jumpsuit held ten strings in one hand. Each string was connected to a Sleeper who floated in the air, trailing slightly behind as the bear pulled them along, like a bouquet of balloons.

"Headed for the Flying Line," Anyway explained.

A group of men dressed in dark suits—one of whom looked alarmingly like Abraham Lincoln—passed by. Taylor Swift followed behind, texting on her smartphone. There were large talking animals, a couple of unicorns, several dentists, a robot that looked like it had been made from tin cans and a giant toaster, and a green-faced witch. These "people" were chatting with each other and laughing, and several of them held paper coffee cups with plastic tops. Stella got the distinct impression that they were headed to work. The Sleepers did not seem to notice any of them. "They work in the dreams. We have an outstanding casting department,"

Anyway said. "Ah! There it is—that's the track you're looking for." He pointed.

When she looked, Stella saw a tunnel marked "The Track You're Looking For."

"Well, that's . . . convenient," she said.

A train was just pulling onto the platform. The locomotive was strangely shaped, rounded at the front. It reminded Stella of a submarine. Sleepers lined the platform, and just as she neared the second car, the doors rattled open.

"Go on," Anyway urged when she hesitated. With a deep breath, she stepped forward and into the car. Inside, it was old-fashioned and elegant, with wood paneling and large windows. The ceiling was made of glass and the bench-like seats were upholstered with red velvet and all faced forward, like seats on a school bus. Several Sleepers had taken seats already. Most sat facing a window, but when Stella looked out, all she saw was the platform she had come from.

"Welcome to the Water Line," announced a tinny voice over the loudspeaker. "Origin stop: Fountain in the Middle of Nowhere. Next stop: Stream."

The train chuffed and rumbled, and then, with a jerk, moved forward. Stella looked down at the papers in her hand. There wasn't much on them: a sketch of a dragon, a fragment from a poem, a sentence that didn't lead anywhere.

"We need a map," Anyway announced. He had to repeat himself twice before Stella managed to tear her eyes away from the pages.

"What?" she asked.

"We need to look at a map."

"You don't know where we're going?"

Anyway's silver whiskers flushed a deep shade of scarlet, and he stuck his nose in the air. "I suppose you know much more about it than I do," he snapped.

"I didn't—"

"No, no, please—go ahead without me, I'm sure you'll be much better off."

"I'm sorry! I didn't mean to insult you."

"Who's insulted? Not I! To be questioned—"

"I never said—"

"—on the Dreamway—"

"I was just—"

"—when I'm but a lowly Door Mouse with only four hundred fifty-seven years of service—"

"Four hundred fifty-seven?" Stella repeated, impressed.

The mouse seemed pleased by her tone. "Yes," he replied. "I know it's but a trifle compared to *your* vast knowledge. . . ."

Stella could see that the mouse wasn't going to be happy until she had flattered him a little. "I didn't realize I was dealing with such an expert."

Anyway's tail flicked impatiently. "Well, you *are*."

"Four hundred and fifty-seven years of service," Stella went on, "certainly means that you know your stuff."

Anyway snorted. "Unlike *some* people," he agreed. "Though I won't say who. Or *What*," he added, emphasizing his nemesis's name.

"So if you say that we should look at a map, then we should," Stella went on. "Absolutely."

"Well, I'm glad that you're going to take my recommendation." Anyway twirled his whiskers. "Finally."

"Where is the map?"

"There's one right there." He pointed toward the nearest door with the tip of his tail. Beside the door was a map behind glass. "They keep them locked up. 'Too volatile,' they say. But I like to keep my own." He pulled something from the pouch around his neck, and unfolded it twenty-seven times, until it was a full-size map.

"Oh," Stella said as she glanced at the map, for she could see at once that it was a mad tangle of lines that seemed to shift and change with every glance. She looked down at Anyway, who was haughtily inspecting his tail, as if the entire matter was beneath him. "Could you please tell me how to read this map?"

The little mouse harrumphed. "It changes according to who is in it," he said with a huff.

"That doesn't make any sense!"

"Of course it does. The same thing happens in your world, doesn't it?"

"What? No! In my world, things stay the same no matter who's there and who isn't!"

"Really?" Anyway replied. "When people leave, things don't change?" And the way he said it made

Stella think of her father. Her mother didn't laugh as often when he wasn't around, and Cole got into trouble more than he normally did. She couldn't prove it, but even the weather seemed to be worse when he was gone.

"Please help me, Anyway," Stella said at last.

"Fine," he snapped. He peered over the edge of her pocket and stared at the map. His whiskers tickled her cheek, but she strained to keep herself from giggling. She didn't want to offend the mouse again. She didn't have that kind of time. "We're on the Water Line . . . here's Memory . . . ah, let's avoid Humiliation Line . . . hm—hum!" He muttered to himself for a few minutes until he finally sat up straight, announcing, "Got it! We'll need to make three transfers, but we'll get there."

"Where are we going?"

"We need to find out just where your brother is. The Nightmare Line has more than one station, after all. So we'll stop in to see a friend of mine."

The lights flickered, then went out with a sudden, shocking blackness. Stella felt the brakes engage and smelled the acrid burn as the train slowed. Overhead, the lights buzzed and flickered on. The brakes screeched as the train stopped. It paused a moment, as if it were catching its breath, and then the doors snapped open.

When she looked around, Stella saw that the train was empty. "Anyway?" she called.

Wait, she thought, *should I get off here? The mouse said we would transfer. Did he mean now? Did he get off already?* "Anyway!"

She was afraid to get off of the train without him, and she was just as afraid to stay on it. Already, the voice was announcing the station stop. There was nothing beyond the doors—at least nothing Stella could see. . . .

"Last call," said the voice over the loudspeaker. "Next stop—"

"Anyway!" There was no reply. The doors began to rattle, and Stella darted through them.

"Mind the gap," said the voice as Stella fell from the platform and landed with a splash.

THE GREEN MAN

STELLA FOUND HERSELF ON HER knees as water splashed and played around her, giggling as it rolled past. Overhead, light filtered through branches with yellow and orange leaves. She stood up, taking in the forest. A chipmunk sat on a nearby log. Red toadstools with white spots grew nearby, vibrant among delicate green ferns. It was picturesque to say the least, the kind of enchanting woodland favored by captive princesses and dancing woodchucks. And there—just visible among the ferns—was a smooth white pebble. Stella dragged her wet feet from the stream, her soaked pajama bottoms clinging to her legs as she made her way to the pebble. She picked it up and held it in her hand. It took her a moment to spot the next one—it was about ten feet away, near a stump.

"I know this place," Stella whispered to herself. It was the forest from her book of fairy tales. The white pebbles . . . they were the ones Hansel and Gretel had left behind on their first trip to the forest where the wicked witch lived.

Something rustled, and Stella wheeled around. "Who's that?" she demanded. There was silence for a moment, then more rustling. Sound is always louder and more terrifying when one is alone in a forest, and Stella judged the thing in the bushes to be roughly the size of a rhinoceros. A moment later, the thing came crashing through a bush. She threw the pebble at it, and Anyway cried, "Ouch!"

Stella staggered backward a step as the mouse glared at her. "You scared me," she said, feeling foolish.

The mouse rubbed his forehead. "Oh, well, I'm very sorry for your troubles, that's to be sure," he said sarcastically. "Being startled is a good reason to throw a boulder at someone, of course."

"It was only a pebble," Stella replied.

Anyway pointed to the rock. "It's the size of my head!"

Stella winced. "Well, I *am* sorry. Really. And I'm very glad to see you. Where were you?"

"You've landed in a dream," Anyway told her. "I hadn't counted on that. You're not a Sleeper, after all. I wasn't sure what would happen when the train stopped, to tell you the truth."

"Where are the others?" Stella asked.

"Oh, they're off having their own dreams," Anyway said vaguely. "They're around here somewhere, but on another level, as it were. We can't see them; they can't see us. But I'm sure a few of them got off here."

"Which is—where, exactly?"

"Look, the Dreamway runs on tracks. Each line has a different name. Right now, you're on the Water line— stops are Ocean, Pool, Rain—"

"Stream?" Stella guessed, looking back at the flowing water behind her. "So—if this is a dream, then what was that train?"

"Look, when you go to a restaurant, you sit down and order a meal, right? And everyone gets something different to eat—whatever they ordered. But the restaurant is more than just the meal. It's the waiters, it's the tablecloths. And there's more that you never really see and don't think much about—like everything in the kitchen. So I thought—seeing as how you're not exactly a customer of this particular restaurant—we could just scoot around with the cooks and waiters. But now we've ended up at a table, with an order of steak."

Inhaling deeply, Stella took a look around. The forest smelled sweet, almost like cinnamon, and she wondered if that was the scent of the witch's gingerbread house nearby. "I think it's more like dessert."

"Whatever. Point is you're not quite a waiter, not quite a customer, but I guess we've got to eat this forest before we transfer."

"I'm not sure that metaphor is working, exactly," Stella said.

"So Water intersects with other lines—Memory, for example. It even intersects with the Nightmare Line. That's Drowning, that is, usually," Anyway said. He curled his silver tail around his front paws and gazed at her with a serious expression.

"Usually?"

Anyway twitched his whiskers. "You saw how things change around here. My friend is at Ocean— that's where we're headed next. So let's just get through this and on to the next stop."

"Okay."

They stared at each other for a moment.

"Er . . ." Anyway said finally. "This is your dream. So I'm not really in charge here."

"Oh."

"Any ideas?"

Stella looked around. "I think . . . I think I'm in Hansel and Gretel," she admitted. "In a scene from a storybook in my world."

"Ah, well, that's possible." Anyway said.

"I . . . think I should follow these pebbles . . ." Stella looked around. One lay to her left, and one lay to her right. There was no way to know which one had been put down first. "But . . . which way?"

Anyway looked thoughtfully at the stone that had bopped him on the head.

"Hey, whippersnappers!" screeched a tiny voice,

and when she looked up, she saw something green wiggling on a branch. It was an inchworm, and a rather fat one at that. "Get off my lawn, or I'll call my lawyer!"

"What's wrong with him?" Stella asked.

"Meh." Anyway shrugged. "Who knows? Dreams." And he shook his head and chuckled.

"I'll sue you!" the inchworm bellowed. "I'll sue you and I'll sue everyone who has ever met you! I'll sue this branch you're standing on and I'll sue the leaves for standing by and refusing to stop this injustice—"

"Excuse me—"

"Please do not interrupt, little girl, I'm preparing my case!"

"But, um, we're leaving."

"Not fast enough!" the inchworm complained. "Taking your time about it, aren't you?" He gazed at her with yellow eyes that had no pupils. They were like solid marbles. "Well, it isn't hard to take *your* measure."

"What?" Stella was very confused, which was not a feeling she liked. She was used to understanding things, and this dream was irritating her.

"*What? What?*" he sneered in a high-pitched voice. "Pretty awake, aren't you? For someone in a dream? Looking for something, are you?"

"Pebbles," Stella told him.

"No, that's not it." The inchworm shook his head (which was rather like waving the entire top half of his body). "You need to find the Green Man."

"The Green Man?" Stella repeated.

"He's gobbled up what you're looking for!" The inchworm looked into the distance just over her shoulder. "That direction!" Then he inched away. Stella supposed that he was trying to be haughty and that this was his version of storming off. But it takes a long time for an inchworm to get anywhere, and so she and Anyway rather awkwardly watched him until he was gone.

"What do you think?" Anyway asked once the inchworm had disappeared into a small hole in the tree.

"I guess we should go find the Green Man," Stella said. Anyway nodded. "He said that direction—and there's a pebble, so . . ." She hesitated. "But he said it had *gobbled up* what I was looking for—"

"Well," Anyway looked thoughtful, twirling his whiskers like a long moustache, "I'm sure that's not as bad as it sounds."

★

The stream flowed over smooth stones beside a moss-covered riverbank. The water hissed and rushed, turning white in the places it swirled from stone to stone. Brooks are often said to be babblers, but Stella was beginning to suspect that this one was more of a gossip. It had heard some very scandalous things about the inchworm, and was more than delighted to tell Anyway all about it. At least, this was what Anyway explained to Stella as they walked along, collecting white pebbles. She couldn't understand what the stream was saying and only heard Anyway's side of the conversation, which was mostly composed of, "oh *no*" and "and *then* what happened?" and "go *on*." The trees reached their long branches overhead, occasionally dripping yellow leaves, which floated in melancholy paths to the forest floor.

The air was sweet and still smelled of cinnamon but of living earth, too, and the forest seemed composed of images from every story Stella had ever read. There was a thin circle of tiny blue mushrooms on frail stalks, like a fairy ring. There was a stand of birches with their paper-curling bark. And over there, far in the distance, Stella caught sight of colorful puffballs on long stems: truffula trees.

Stella was not sure that she wanted to meet the Green Man, whoever he was. An ogre, perhaps. Or a leprechaun. Or, less likely but still frightening, a Martian. It was a dream, after all, wasn't it? The Green Man could be *anything*. She only knew one thing about him, and that was that he had gobbled up something.

None of this seemed promising.

"Really?" Anyway said to the stream. "I don't believe it!"

"Now what's the stream saying?" Stella asked.

"It's not fit for your ears!" Anyway whispered. "But that inchworm is really quite a rascal—oh!" This last syllable made Stella look up, and Anyway hissed, "There he is."

A large mass of moss-covered rock rose from the earth. Bushes and ivy grew thick across and at the top, having spread in such a way that it seemed to make long hair, two eyes, and a nose over an open, gaping mouth. Three white pebbles stood out like snow on a mountaintop as they led the way into the maw. The eyes gazed darkly at her.

"It's a cave," Stella whispered. "The Green Man is a cave."

"Well," Anyway said brightly, "I told you that gobbling thing probably wasn't as bad as it sounded."

With a few steps, she passed through into the mouth of the Green Man. The walls glittered with gems, sparkling gently—a rock's equivalent of a whisper. It was a sacred place, and Stella felt the rocks' reverence. She thought they might, perhaps, be curious about her and what she was doing there. One of them twinkled, almost like a wink.

"It's so beautiful," Stella said.

Anyway shrugged. "They're just rocks."

She took a few more steps, and her heart clunked. She was struck with the sudden fear that the mouth would close, trapping her inside. The moment she thought this, she wished she hadn't, because the idea grew and grew until it became the only thought in her mind.

But she did not have to journey far to find what she was looking for. Only a few steps in, reflecting the light that poured in from the mouth of the cave, was a smooth pool of water about the size of the rug in her room at home. Somehow, in the way we know things in dreams, she knew for certain that it was deep—*very* deep. It gleamed like silver, and as Stella drew near, she saw something floating near the center. It was a piece of paper. She knelt to look at it more closely. A piece of notebook paper . . . on it, she saw several lines in very familiar handwriting.

She gasped. "It's Cole's! *The darkness came for me,*" she read the words on the scrap aloud.

Anyway scrambled out of her pocket and down her arm, dropping to the cool floor of the cave. He stared for a moment and then looked up at her.

"My brother was *here,*" Stella said, and she reached for the paper.

"Wait, don't!" Anyway shouted as a green hand burst out of the water and grabbed Stella by the wrist, yanking her forward, pulling her into the water, and down, down, down.

Deep in the Dream
The Darkness came for me
With invisible claws,
Pulled me down
Until falling felt the same
As standing still,
And I had no breath to scream or cry
Until . . .

Stella fell to the floor with a crash. It took her a moment to understand the wood beneath her, the book digging into her rib cage.

This was her room. *Her* room. Her mother was still on the bed, asleep on her side, her back to Stella.

Stella put a hand to her head. *What happened?* she asked herself. She had read the beginning of Cole's poem, and then it was like she fell into it. As if the poem had pulled her into the space between dreaming and being awake, and then all the way through.

Stella rolled to her knees and pushed herself toward the lamp on her side table. She blinked in the sudden light.

I was just dreaming, she told herself. The stillness of the quiet apartment was suddenly cut with her brother's snore. She had often complained about it in the past, but now Stella felt comforted by the familiar sound. *Cole is fine,* she told herself. *He's dreaming too.* Stella climbed beneath the comforter on her bed, tucking herself beneath it. She clicked off the lamp and lay there, staring up at the ceiling and listening to her mother's steady breath. She was not sleepy, not even a little. Her heart pounded in her chest, shaking her whole body like an earthquake, or a rumbling train.

THE LIBRARY

THE WALK TO SCHOOL THE next morning found Stella feeling like a cake that had been taken out of the oven just a few minutes too soon. After breakfast, her heart felt light and poufy, but as the morning wore on, her mood sank, and then settled into a gooey crater.

Her mother had gushed over the birthday gift Stella made her—it was a page-a-day calendar that had taken Stella weeks to put together. On each day was a quote about motherhood, or love, or the value of hugs, or something kind of borderline soppy like that. Stella had also marked all of the national holidays and family holidays (like Aunt Gertie's birthday), and she had done it all with colored pencils and she had drawn little hearts and flowers on each page. It was a practical gift, which was important to Stella. Her mother would have loved anything—Stella and Cole often joked that they could probably give her a used tissue and she would go out and frame it—but Stella liked things to be *useful*.

As predicted, her mother burst into tears, gave her a big hug, and flipped through the calendar until she came to the page for her anniversary, and then she cried even more.

"Did—did Dad ever call back?" Stella asked.

"Honey, he just called yesterday," Tamara pointed out. Then she wiped her palms across her face and announced, "I'll keep this forever." Although she said the same thing every year, it was still gratifying, and that was what made Stella feel like a fluffy cake of happiness.

Cole didn't have a gift. "I wrote you a poem," he said. His eyebrows drew together and he blinked, as if the kitchen light pained him. "But I can't—I can't find my notebook."

Stella flinched. It was as if Cole had said, "I can't find my right leg." Strangely, though, he didn't seem that upset about it.

"Are you okay?" Tamara leaned over and felt his forehead in the style of mothers everywhere.

"I feel pretty bad," Cole admitted. "Kinda . . . foggy."

"You don't have a fever," Tamara said. "I've got class this morning. I think you'd better go to school, but have the nurse call me if you feel worse, okay?"

Cole's dark, blank eyes blinked. He nodded.

He hadn't said another word as they walked to the subway. He looked absolutely green as they rode, but when Stella asked if he was okay, he snapped, "I'm *fine*."

But he wasn't fine. Stella could feel waves of negative energy coming off him. It was like he was radioactive. And so, bit by bit, the air seeped out of her happiness cake.

They climbed the stairs out of the subway and headed up the street. They turned a corner and started up a slow hill. This was one thing Stella appreciated about their school. It was uphill on the way there and downhill on the way home, when you were tired.

Fog had settled on the city, and droplets of moisture collected on Stella's lashes, making her eyes water.

It was a spring day that looked comparatively warm according to the thermometer, but actually felt quite cold. The damp air settled over her, seeping through her insides, until a shiver took over to shake her up.

They passed by a block of row houses—all ugly things, with metal awnings and exhausted-looking siding. On the next block, Angry Pete stood near his fence with a mug of what could, conceivably, be coffee. "Stop looking at me," he muttered as they passed. "Just don't look at me."

As usual, Stella edged closer to her brother, but she felt him stiffen beside her. "Shut *up*," he snarled.

"Cole!" Stella was shocked, but he didn't pause in his stride, just stomped away, head bent forward, eyes on the ground. Cole hardly ever got mad, and when he did, it was always a surprise. This seemed to have come out of nowhere.

Stella turned back, but Angry Pete didn't notice. He just kept muttering to himself. He wore his usual sweatpants and heavy work boots. Stella noticed that his shoes had paint on them. It had never occurred to her before to wonder what he did for a living, but she supposed he was a house painter. She wondered if it was hard for him to find work. She wondered if he lived by himself. She wondered if he had trouble paying his rent.

She wondered why he was so angry.

Turning back to her brother, she saw that Cole had not stopped walking or even slowed down. It was a struggle to catch him, and it made her irritable. "What's the matter with you?" she demanded.

"I'm sick of people messing with me. I want to be more like Dad." He glared over his shoulder and spat.

"Dad?" Her father never snapped at anyone. "What are you talking about?"

"Dad. *Dad*," he repeated, as if maybe she was hard of hearing. "Used to live with us? Rolls around the desert in a Jeep with a rifle, looking for IEDs? *Dad*."

"He—" She never thought of her father that way. Not even once, the entire time he had been deployed. Not even when she saw pictures of him in his gear. Her father was an electrical engineer. He liked to cook lasagna. He would sit on the bed and read to her—he had a great reading voice. She could picture him at a desk, or at a pool, or on a roller coaster. But, even though he was a Marine reservist, she never pictured him as a soldier. Never. "That's not Dad," she said finally. What she meant was that it wasn't the Dad part of him, just some other, separate part.

"Yes, it is," Cole answered. And then—so fast that she couldn't be sure—she thought she saw him flicker.

They walked the rest of the way in silence.

By the time she was a block from Stringwood, Stella remembered something: today's Spirit Day theme was the 1960s. Kids were dressed in bell-bottom jeans and flowered shirts, or T-shirts with peace signs. Some of them wore bandannas and little round-framed sunglasses. Stella sighed. She had on her regular clothes. At this point, her fluffy cake of happiness was basically a pancake. One that had been repeatedly run over by heavy machinery.

As she sat in French, Stella glanced out the window. Bleu's nest was there, but the bird was not. Stella knew that this didn't mean anything—she didn't see Bleu every single day—but his absence left her with the same unsettled feeling she'd had when she heard her father still hadn't called. She tried not to look out at the gingko tree, which stood dripping and solitary beneath the gray sky. When the bell rang, Stella's body automatically went to her locker, got her lunch bag, moved toward the cafeteria. But her mind was noticing strange things. A chip in the paint that looked like a mushroom, the flabby porridge color of the walls, the odd smell of rot that seemed as if it were coming from the back of her nostrils.

"Are you okay?" Renee asked as she caught up to Stella in the hallway. The corridors were the usual crush and jumble of bodies trying to get to classes.

"I'm fine," Stella said. "Why?"

"Um, because you're walking the wrong way?" Renee asked. "Like, I have no idea what class you're going to now, unless your next class is in the cafeteria."

Stella stopped and looked. Renee was right—her body had somehow skipped her next class and gone straight to lunch.

"No offense, but you've been seriously spaced out today," Renee told her.

"I have?" Stella asked.

Renee folded her arms across her chest. "Um, first,

we said we were both going to wear peasant dresses, and instead, you're wearing a T-shirt with a cat on it."

"Well," Stella said, looking down at her shirt, "it's a cartoon cat."

"*How is that from the 1960s? And then* I told you that I have two cavities, and you were like, 'That's great; I've never been there.'" She twisted her lips to the side of her mouth. "I let it go because half the time I don't listen to you, either, but now I'm starting to wonder."

"Half the time you don't listen to me?"

"Stella! I'm your best friend! I don't have to listen to you *all* the time. Anyway, this isn't about me—it's about you and why you're acting like you're broadcasting via satellite. What's up? And by the way, we'd better start moving, or we'll be late." Renee hitched her bag higher onto her shoulders and turned in the direction of the gym.

"I just—I had this really weird dream last night," Stella admitted. She felt still coated with the ugly scum that the dream had left on her.

"Ohmygosh! Me, too!"

"Really? I dreamed I was traveling through this

subway system and I had to find my way out—"

"That's just like my dream!"

"You're kidding!" Stella gaped at her friend.

"Yes!" Renee pushed her purple-framed glasses up farther onto her nose and looked very serious. "I dreamed I was stuck in a chocolate chip cookie and had to eat my way out."

"What? That's not the same thing at all," Stella replied.

"Well, we were both trapped." Renee was a little huffy.

"That's—that's—" Well, Stella wasn't sure what it was. She didn't know how she could possibly communicate the way the Dreamway had made her feel, or how it had made her afraid for her brother. "Okay, you're right," she said finally. "They're totally alike."

Renee squeezed Stella around the shoulders, reaching awkwardly to avoid her backpack. Then she stood firmly in front of Stella and looked at her closely. Her warm brown eyes were serious. She said, "I really do know what you mean, though. I've had that kind of dream. The kind where you wake up, and you think you're still in it. And then, when you realize you aren't, you're just so grateful."

"I *still* feel like I'm in it, though," Stella admitted.

"But you're not." Renee gestured to the gray lockers that lined the hallway on either side of them. "You're here, with me, at Stringwood. And nothing weird ever happens at Stringwood."

Three kids wearing long-haired wigs scurried past them. The tallest boy handed Renee a daisy and said, "Stay groovy, man! Channel your flower power!" The other two laughed and kept walking.

"Except for that," Renee added. "That just happened, and it was kind of weird."

The traffic in the hallway was thinning out. A girl in a hoodie raced past—it was the quiet pause just before the bell, where the few remaining stragglers flitted like dragonflies to get to class. But the two girls remained face-to-face, stock still in the hallway.

"We need to go," Stella said.

"It's gym; I'll just change fast," Renee replied. "I want to make sure you're okay."

"I'm okay," Stella told her.

"Really?"

"Yes," Stella promised. *I'm in the real world*, she told herself. *There's only one real world, and this is it.* This thought was so encouraging that her brain even added, *Stay groovy.*

She resolved to try.

★

"That's not going to work." Renee stared at the rope dangling from a hook in the ceiling of the gym. They were supposed to try to climb up it. It would, according to their teacher, Coach Thuy, build their upper body strength. Renee looked at Stella. "Not happening."

"Nope," Stella agreed. Her stomach felt scooped out and hollow as she remembered what it had felt like the night before to have a hand and a leg that actually worked.

"Coach!" Renee called. "Excuse me!" She waved her hand and Ms. Thuy turned her head. She was young and had a ponytail, but she was tough. She had a silver whistle, and she knew how to use it. Ms. Thuy lifted an eyebrow, and Renee grabbed Stella's hand and dragged her over.

"Stella can't do the rope," Renee announced.

"*Renee*," Stella snapped, giving her friend a little elbow in the ribs.

The coach looked thoughtfully at Stella's right arm for a moment. It was her job to be encouraging and to have kids push their limits, but even she could see that, sometimes, real life is different from a TV movie. "Your brother wasn't feeling well, either. He's on his way to the library."

"Could I go too?"

"Sure." Coach Thuy reached into her pocket and pulled out a small pad. She scribbled a note and tore it off. "See you tomorrow."

Stella and Renee gave their crooked-finger lock, and Stella pushed through the doors and headed, solo, down the hall to the library.

The library wasn't elegant. The wooden tables were scuffed and ugly, and most of the chairs wobbled. Many of the books were old and some had clearly endured a rough life of snack spills and internment at the bottom of backpacks. But the library had two features that were the pride and joy of Ethel B. Stringwood School:

a row of brand-new computers and, located on the wall behind the librarian's desk, a vibrant mosaic—a beautiful silver mirrored bridge over the blue tile waves of a river.

As far as Stella was concerned, the librarian, Ms. Slaughter, was the library's third remarkable feature. Quiet but kind, she was a young mother whose desk was covered with photos of her four-year-old son, who apparently wore a mouse costume more or less constantly. She seemed to have read every book in the library and could always recommend just the right thing. When Stella came in, Mrs. Slaughter gave her a smile. She accepted the note and nodded. "Anywhere you like."

A student with long black hair was already at the row of computers, tapping away. Stella walked over and sat down beside her. "Hey, Alice," she said as Alice looked up.

"Oh, hi." With a quick tap, she minimized the window on-screen and smiled at Stella. "No gym today?"

"Rope climbing." Stella sighed.

Alice nodded. This would have been her physical education period, too, but instead, she had a permanent study hall.

"Hey—" Stella hauled her backpack onto her lap and unzipped it. The plastic jar of peanut butter was at the top, and she pulled it out.

"Thanks!" Alice said, taking it from her. "You remembered!"

"Renee did."

"I'll stick it in the box." She tossed it into the book bag slung across the back of her wheelchair.

"Have you seen Cole?" Stella asked. Alice looked blank, so Stella added, "My brother?"

"Oh—right. No, I haven't," Alice told her. "But I've had my back to the door."

Stella said thanks and headed off, wandering between rows of shelves. She didn't see Cole anywhere. After trying a few more rows, she noticed that a white wooden door in the corner was ajar. It was the stairs that led to the stacks in the subbasement. These stairs were narrow, with a railing made of metal pipe and peeling paint. Stella took the stairs.

The stacks smelled of old paper and slow thoughts. They were small, taking up roughly half the space of the floor above, and cramped, with a ceiling that seemed to press down, hulking low. Stella didn't have to crouch to move through the space, but she felt as if she did.

She couldn't see Cole, but she could hear someone at the back of the stacks. Something was hitting the wall. *Thunk, thunk, thunk*, then three lighter taps. *Tink, tink, tink.*

She crept through the towering books and saw her brother's back as he pounded on the wall. It was him—his particular slouchy stance, his wrinkled Ironman shirt (Cole had forgotten about Spirit Day too)—but his movements were jerky and awkward. It was him, but he was strange. He pounded his fist against the wall again and stood there.

The wall pounded back.

Thunk, thunk, thunk. Somewhere, in the darkness beyond the wall, something was answering.

Stella's heart was slow, her blood was thick,

everything in her body seemed clogged. She took a careful step backward and then another. Finally, she turned and hurried away, up the stairs, back toward the illumination of the library. But as she burst from the narrow stairwell, she ran into a library cart, knocking a dozen or more books from the top shelf.

"Are you okay?" Ms. Slaughter hurried to her side as Stella stumbled to her feet.

"I'm—" Stella looked over her shoulder at the white door. There was no sign of Cole. Was he still down there? "I'm fine."

Ms. Slaughter looked at her carefully, and Stella tried to appear normal, but something was happening to her hearing—her ears felt full of cotton, her vision was narrowing.

The librarian put a gentle hand on Stella's arm. "Are you sure?" she asked gently. She shifted, and one of the overhead lights lit up her green eyes. Stella had the feeling of the woods and the eyes of the Green Man.

Stella's heart felt sluggish, her throat wheezed. Dark mist swirled in from everywhere, narrowing her vision, then blurring it. She was aware that Ms. Slaughter was speaking; she was aware of movement, but she couldn't see it, couldn't hear it. . . .

She fell into a deep, dark lake of shadows. As she fell, she saw a small silver mouse skitter across the smooth black soil on the shore. It meant something, that mouse, but she didn't know what. Darkness covered her vision and she couldn't connect her thoughts—it was as if the shadows had leaked in through her ears, fogging her brain. She felt someone take her hand. It was as if her whole body had been caught by one of those large metal claws in a midway game, and like a dusty teddy bear, she felt herself jerked upward.

"Stella?"

"Stella?"

Stella looked up into Alice's worried face. Her eyes were green—no, they were black. Stella was lying on the floor.

"Um—this is embarrassing," Stella said.

"What happened?" Alice asked. She looked over at the librarian, who shook her head to indicate that she had no idea.

Stella sat up.

"You need to go to the nurse," Ms. Slaughter told her. "You fainted."

Stella blinked as the mist around her cleared slowly—Stella remembered where she was. It was the library.

She didn't bother correcting Ms. Slaughter. Stella knew what had happened—she'd had a seizure. An absence seizure. She hadn't had one in a long time; the medicine was supposed to stop them.

"Can you stand up?" The librarian held out a dimpled hand.

Stella tried her legs and discovered that they worked. She scanned the floor for signs of a silvery gray mouse, but there were none. There was no sign of Cole, either.

"Take my arm," Ms. Slaughter said. She picked up Stella's hand and placed it into the crook of her elbow. "Can you walk?" She guided Stella toward the narrow elevator, half-hidden beside the librarian's tiny office.

As she stood in the elevator, she caught Alice's gaze. Her face was pale, her eyes wide. She clutched a notebook to her chest like a shield.

Stella's mind still felt obscure and saturated, as if it had been soaked in ink.

"You'll be fine, you just need to rest," Ms. Slaughter said. "Have you eaten lunch yet?"

Stella looked blank. "No," she admitted. "I have lunch next period."

"That's it, then. You just need to eat and lie down." The librarian patted her hand.

There was still no sign of Cole as the elevator door slid shut.

BACK AT HOME

STELLA STILL FELT LOUSY LATER that evening. The seizure had left her exhausted, and she decided that the best thing would be to simply veg out on the couch for a while. The living room flickered in the pale blue light from the television. "I thought you hated this show," Stella said as she sat down on the green couch beside Cole.

Cole cocked his head and looked carefully at the television screen. With a shrug, he changed the channel. He rubbed his forehead, then handed Stella the remote. "You want to pick something else? I'm going to lie down."

"Still feel terrible?" Stella asked.

Cole looked at her, and for a moment there was a

flame in his eyes—like a flare from a ship on a dark sea. He was about to say something, Stella felt sure of it, something important. But the moment passed, his gaze fuzzed—a window fogged with cold. In the end, he said, "Just a headache."

When he stood up, Stella noticed that he didn't smell like himself. There was a strange scent coming off of him that reminded her of something. Of fall leaves a few days after a rain. The scent had lingered at the back of her nostrils earlier that day.

"Cole—I—" He stared through her, and for a moment, she imagined that she could see dust motes swirling in the space where he stood. "What were you doing in the library?"

The was just a moment, a brief pause, before he said, "What?"

"During PE I saw you in the stacks, and—"

His eyes narrowed. "Were you following me?" Stella stood frozen as he closed the distance between them.

"Don't follow me!" he yelled the words right at her,

his breath hot on her face. Then he turned and lumbered off toward his room.

For a moment, Stella stood there in shock. Fear settled onto her chest, a cold weight, as she tried to make sense of Cole's un-Cole actions.

Tamara appeared at the doorway. "What happened? I heard yelling. Where's your brother? Are you okay?"

"He went to lie down," Stella replied. "And I'm . . . fine."

Tamara glanced in the direction of Cole's door. With a sigh, she stepped into the living room and sank into a navy wingchair. She closed her eyes and tipped her head backward.

"I begged Nurse Amy not to call you," Stella said. "I told her it was no big deal."

Her mother's eyes opened, but she didn't turn her head. "I know," she said to the ceiling. "Maybe you're coming down with something."

"It's only a seizure," Stella said. "They're not dangerous."

Her mother's eyes closed again, and Stella knew

what she was thinking of: the first time—the worst time—that Stella had gotten sick. Stella didn't remember, because she was only two at the time, but she'd had a stroke. Cole had noticed that something was wrong. He'd toddled over to James and announced, "Stella not right."

Stella had been in the hospital for seven days. She didn't remember it, but sometimes she felt as if her mother had never gotten over it.

"I know the seizures themselves aren't dangerous." Tamara turned her head against the back of the chair to look at Stella. "But you could fall or hit your head—"

"The library is carpeted."

"That's lucky."

Her mother didn't ask why she was in the library in the first place, and Stella didn't explain. She didn't want to talk about it.

The doorbell rang and the door burst open as Aunt Gertie barreled through, singing out, "Here I am! Here I am!" A moment later, she appeared in the living room, her curly black hair and pink jacket dappled with rain. Renee was right behind her, carrying a bakery box.

When she saw Stella on the couch, Aunt Gertie let out her familiar laugh—the hoot of a small, cheerful owl. "Hoo-hoo! You look like a queen, all propped up on your pillows."

"Oh, Mom, leave her alone," Renee said. "She's had a traumatic event!"

"It really wasn't that big of a deal," Stella insisted as Aunt Gertie bent to give her a kiss. A delicious smell wafted up from the paper shopping bag in Gertie's right hand. "I brought you . . ." she announced in her musical Cape Verde accent, ". . . some delicious food all the way from China. Hoo-hoo-hoo!"

"More like China Garden," Renee put in.

"Even better," Tamara said.

"And you!" Aunt Gertie wheeled on her best friend. "What are you doing there relaxing? Get to work!" She laughed again, showing the gap in her teeth.

Gertie's appearance seemed to buoy Tamara, who stood up to give her friend a hug. "You're a lifesaver," she said.

"I know!" Gertie was already in motion, moving toward the kitchen. Angela trailed after her and soon dinner—General Tso's chicken, mapo tofu, spring rolls, dumplings, wantons, and a few dishes that Stella didn't recognize—appeared on the table. They sat down to eat, and Gertie made everyone smile as she chatted about the owner of the restaurant, Larry Wei. Stella marveled at how Gertie knew everyone, and everyone knew her. "He always gives me a discount," Aunt Gertie said. "He loves me."

"He loves me more," Renee put in.

"That's true!" Aunt Gertie said. "He gives Renee free egg rolls!" She turned to Stella and winked. "Look at her!" Gertie said, hooting. "She is falling asleep at the table!"

"Go to bed," Tamara said gently, so Stella slowly hauled herself out of her chair and dragged her body toward the hallway.

"Okay, I will tuck you in," Gertie said, and she placed her mug of tea on the coffee table and reached for Stella's hand. "Then your mother will come and kiss you good night."

Renee rushed over to give Stella a good-night hug, and Stella let Gertie guide her to her bedroom. She pulled back the covers so that Stella could slide in, then pulled the blanket over her and gave her a kiss on the forehead. She glanced at the calendar beside Stella's bed. "Your father will be home soon," she said gently.

"I know." *Soon*, she repeated to herself. *Soon*.

"Sweet dreams. Dream of beautiful beaches. A nice vacation for your Mom, okay?"

"Thanks, Aunt Gertie," Stella said, rolling over onto her side and closing her eyes. "Would you say good-night to Cole for me?" she asked sleepily.

"Cole?" Aunt Gertie repeated, almost as if she had forgotten about him or had never heard the name before.

Stella rolled back over to ask about it, but the mattress dipped and swayed, like a waterbed, and she became aware of a strange sound. It was like small waves lapping against a shore. She sat up, and her bed rocked beneath her. "Keep steady," said a voice, and Stella let out a scream.

Aunt Gertie was gone, but Stella was not alone.

"Oh. Eep, a mouse," Anyway droned. He rolled his eyes in annoyance. "Help, help, it's going to eat me."

"Where am I?" Stella demanded as the bed shifted and swayed again. Anyway perched on her brass footboard and watched her, head cocked, grinning a very ratty grin.

"Dark Water. Almost at the next station on the Water Line," Anyway told her. "Obviously."

Yes, here she was, in a bed floating on what seemed to be a vast black velvet ocean. In the sky, a full moon rose, casting light that shattered and sparkled across the water. But there was something strange about the moon—instead of its usual silver gray, it was a swirl of green and blue. "Is that—Earth?" Stella asked after a moment.

Anyway turned to look. "Perhaps," he said.

Stella looked down into the water. Tiny pinpoints of fire sparkled in the inky water. "Mare Crisium," Stella murmured, naming one of the oceans on the moon. She thought of the Italian astronomer and wondered what he would make of this. "What am I doing here?" Stella asked herself.

"Don't ask me," Anyway replied. "I just do doorways. And it was no easy job finding one that led right to you, let me tell you. I even thought I had you once—and then you slipped away! Troublesome girl."

"But—what happened?" Stella asked. "I thought it was all a dream!"

"Well, it *was* a dream," Anyway explained. "But it wasn't your dream. It was your brother's."

"How could I end up in his dream?"

"I've been wondering that myself. Perhaps it's because you're twigs?"

Stella thought this over. "Do you mean because we're *twins*?"

"Yes, *obviously* that's what I meant," Anyway snapped. "You caught the Dross—the end of his dream—while it was fading. And then it ended completely and you went back to the Penumbra; sorry, to *the real world*."

"When I found his poem, it was like I was *in* it," she said.

"The poem pulled you into the exit. That's what exits are like. Neither Here nor There, just a sense of things." Anyway looked over his shoulder. "Well! It looks like we're coming right up to it!"

"Up to what?"

"Up to where we're going."

Stella looked about her. They were simply bobbing like a cork in the water. "It's going to take forever to get anywhere—we're in the middle of a dream ocean!"

"It isn't really a dream ocean," the mouse corrected. "It's part of the Dreamway. We're close to a station. The hub of the Water Line, in fact, and besides . . ." He cleared his throat. "You *do* have an oar."

Stella saw that this was, in fact, correct. Lying across her lap was a wooden oar. She sighed. "All right," she said at last. "Tell me which way to go."

OCEAN

Anyway was right—Stella paddled, and it wasn't long until they came to a series of tall, dark buildings. The waterway stretched between them, like a street, and Anyway directed Stella between the long-legged edifices that resembled water bugs beneath a cold gray sky. There were lights on in the buildings and curtains at the windows, but Stella didn't see any people.

After several turns, they came to a tunnel, and Anyway directed her inside to a dock. She used a sheet to tie up her brass headboard to a cleat on the dock and followed Anyway up a steep ramp. They came out into a large, wide-open space with a domed ceiling made of glass. It looked onto miles of ocean from far below the surface. Light filtered softly through the water, rippling on the gray floor of the station. It reminded Stella of the large tank she had seen at the aquarium two summers before. A cloud of silver fish, each as long as her finger, floated past her on the air inside the station.

"Breeze fish," Anyway explained as he watched them for a few moments.

There were many tunnels with tracks leading out of the station, but Anyway avoided those. Instead, he led Stella toward the information booth.

He didn't ask for information, but went around to the back of the booth and pointed to a low door. "Through there," he said, and then scampered inside.

The door only came up to Stella's chest, so she had to duck. She crouched low and hunched forward, feeling the floor descend in a long, low ramp. She went down, down, down, and as she did, the ceiling got higher and higher. A noise came from below that was like the sound of a beehive—the humming of electricity mixed with a metallic rattle. It was only when she came to a metal walkway and looked down that Stella realized they were in a baggage handling area. Acres of conveyor belts stretched out below, lined with crate after crate. Every crate held a single item with no rhyme or reason between them: there was large marble statue, then a single wooden toothpick. Dragonflies flitted among the baggage, landed briefly, and darted off. "Baggage Inspectors," Anyway explained. "Every piece of baggage has to be ticketed and routed."

"Ticketed?"

"Sleepers need a ticket to ride the Dreamway," Anyway explained. "When they come in, they're supposed to declare their baggage and then hand it over. They get a ticket with a destination. The baggage is routed to their dream and shows up there. Baggage is what powers all the lines, light or dark."

"What does that mean?"

Anyway twitched and muttered something about "babysitting" and "history lessons." Then he cleared his throat and began, "A while back, the Dreamway was split into two sections. Light baggage goes to power the pleasant dreams—daydreams, dreams of flying, you know, dreams of strength. The dark baggage goes to make power for the darker stuff—falling, unprepared for a test, those dreams where your teeth all fall out—"

"I didn't know other people had those."

"Oh, yes!" Anyway looked surprised. "*Nondentura*. That's a very popular stop."

"So—nightmares," Stella pressed.

"Well, first there are dark dreams, which are more like...worries," Anyway explained. "That's your mind trying to sort something out. But a Nightmare—that's something else. They have their own line, the Nightmares. They run on an entirely different system. They have...a life of their own."

"But if my brother's on the Nightmare Line, why are we here?"

"I want to get this paper from your brother's notebook tested. Once we do, my friend can tell us *exactly where he is* on the Nightmare Line. Then I can go file my report, and we can go get him."

"Uh, we get him first," Stella corrected. "And *then* you file a report."

Anyway sighed. He darted up Stella's leg, crawled up her shirt and dove into her pocket, reemerging a moment later, one tiny fist held aloft. "Forward," he said. "Toward the Receptacles of Image Determination!"

"Uh, what?"

"Just those big bins over there—we need the dark one." The mouse pointed a tiny finger, and Stella saw what he was talking about. Two cargo containers, one black and one white. Stella hurried down several flights of metal stairs as baggage hummed and rolled through its steady roller coaster around and beneath them. They finally reached the ground level and traveled across the floor to where a tangle of belts angled into the enormous dark box.

A golden glimmer flashed and flickered over the container, now disappearing inside, now darting back out again. It was to this flicker that Anyway called, "Spuddle!" The golden dragonfly stopped in midair, its wings still vibrating. The dragonfly blinked at Anyway and whispered, "Oh, no." He zipped down to face the mouse, casting nervous glances at Stella.

"Uh—this area is for authorized personnel only," Spuddle said quickly. "That is, erm—do you have official clearance for—*this*?" He looked at Stella.

She stared back and was surprised to see that this fly was unlike any other she'd seen. His various parts were made of brass. Beneath his wings, Stella noticed cogs turning and gears spinning. Like clockwork, he ticked with every second that passed.

Stella thought, *Time flies*, and giggled softly to herself.

"Shut it, bug," Anyway snapped. "I've come to collect on the favor you owe me."

The dragonfly hushed him and looked around nervously, but the conveyor belts hummed on, and none of the other golden flecks paused in their work. "What is it that you need?" he hissed.

"Test this," Anyway said, producing the single sheet of paper from Cole's notebook. "I want to see the final destination listed on it."

Spuddle looked horrified. "You're not supposed to have that! That's against the regula—"

"Well, I'm sure Dr. Peavey will be fascinated to hear what happened to a particular silver soup spoon that disappeared from the conveyor belt recently," Anyway prodded, and the dragonfly hushed him again.

"All right, all right! Just a moment! Hand it here." Spuddle took the paper. Then, looking around frantically, he dove toward a particular gray frame. Bins traveled through the frame, and something silver shimmered down on them. The silver shimmer then let out a white pouf of smoke or a black one. If it was white, the bin was sent to the right conveyor system—the one that delivered baggage to the white bin. If the smoke was black, the baggage went to the black bin.

There was a slender space between two baggage buckets, and Spuddle dove into the gray frame with the paper. He dropped it and then darted away to tap at something that vaguely resembled a computer keyboard. The keys had unfamiliar symbols, most of which looked like parts pulled from a watch. The moment the paper went through the machine, the computer monitor lit up. "That's odd," Spuddle said slowly, reading from the screen. "Undisclosed?"

The routing belt stopped moving. The paper shivered and shook as silver powder rained down. The gray frame rattled, and black smoke and sparks spewed from the system, hailing down on the baggage below. "Eeeep!" Spuddle shouted.

Anyway's eyes went wide. "That's unexpected," he whispered.

An alarm screamed, and a voice boomed over the loudspeaker. "Inspectors are on their way. Please be prepared to show your paperwork. Inspectors are on their way. Please be prepared to show your paperwork. Inspectors—"

"What the heck do you think you're doing?" Spuddle screeched as he zipped over to them. "What *was* that thing?"

"A Chimerath pulled her brother through," Anyway shouted. "He's somewhere on the Nightmare Line! Didn't the machine say where?"

Spuddle pulled up short. "No," he said. Then he added, "You have to get out of here."

"Not until I find out just what's going on!" Anyway countered.

"Are you insane? I could lose my job, and if the Inspectors see *that*"—he pointed at Stella—"well, I don't need to tell you what will happen!"

Anyway hesitated.

"I think we'd better listen to this fly," Stella said, aware of how strange the sentence sounded.

"*Dragon*fly!" Spuddle snapped. "Follow me!" He darted along the edge of the wall and came to a metal door. "This way, this way!" Spuddle cried as he whooshed to the right, down an arched hallway. "Here! Here!" He zipped into a room, and the other two followed. "Shut the door!"

The door closed with a *thunk*. Spuddle ducked behind a lamp shaped like Barney the Dinosaur. The entire room was piled high with strange treasure—a juke box, several old Coca-Cola bottles, clothing of all kinds, several candelabras, a bicycle, floor lamps, a Captain America lunchbox, a guitar, a suit of armor, posters for monster movies, rugs, stuffed animals— more than Stella even had time to take in. "What *is* this?" she asked.

"Spuddle, come out from behind that ridiculous lamp, I need to talk to you!" Anyway bellowed. It was really very surprising how loudly he could shout, given that he was a mouse.

With nervous clicks and twitches, Spuddle darted out from behind the large purple dinosaur. "Yes?" he said brightly.

"I've heard that there have been some irregularities," Anyway snapped.

Spuddle hovered in midair. "Irregularities?" His large clockwork eyes blinked and he began to tick faster, like an old-fashioned watch wound too tightly. He let out several nervous hiccups. "I suppose you could say that. We've had . . . less baggage than usual. I think some is . . . vanishing?" He let out a nervous hiccup.

"Is it more than just what the Pirate takes?" Anyway pressed.

"Yes . . . it seems to be . . . well, to me, though no one else seems to care—" He looked over his shoulder and dropped his voice to a whisper. "Someone is taking the light baggage! It's uneven, I tell you—I've filed report after report, but nobody ever replies!" Spuddle *tick-tick-boing*ed worriedly.

"Is the baggage usually even?" Stella asked.

"If anything, there should be slightly more light baggage than dark," Spuddle said. "But now there's more and more dark baggage, and it's more and more powerful—like this thing." He held up Cole's paper.

"Look, Spuddle—her brother is somewhere on the Nightmare Line," Anyway said.

"And we're going to rescue him," Stella announced.

Spuddle gasped so loudly that he actually inhaled a feather from the nearby boa, and had to cough and sputter to spit it out. "You're going to the Nightmare Line?" Spuddle gaped at Anyway.

"Well, unless we think of another option," Anyway said quickly.

Spuddle gasped again, inhaling another feather.

"Maybe hover somewhere else," Anyway suggested.

Hack-hack-hack. "Good idea." Spuddle perched on an empty green Coke bottle. "This has to be reported directly to Dr. Peavey!"

"That's what I was thinking," Anyway agreed.

"No reports until *after* we get my brother," Stella insisted.

"How can we get your brother when we don't know where he is? His paper is marked Undisclosed, remember?" Anyway demanded. "Dr. Peavey will know what that means. We need to see him right away!"

"After the Inspectors leave," Spuddle put in. "I don't want to try to explain this to them."

"I'm sure they'll understand," Stella said. "Won't they want to help—?"

"No," Spuddle replied. "They're huge and made of steel. They fix things or they smash things. That's it."

"We'll move on when they're gone," Anyway agreed.

Frustrated tears rose in Stella's eyes, blurring her vision. As unlikely as it seemed, the mouse and the fly were her only hope of fixing whatever, exactly, had gone wrong. She swallowed and forced herself to breathe. She looked around, desperate to anchor herself to something, to find some meaning that made sense. But it all just looked like junk. "What is this place?"

"This is something I wanted to show you," Spuddle explained. "All of this baggage has been marked Undetermined. Like your paper there."

"So—what?" Stella gaped at the roomful of objects.

"Yes—so what?" Spuddle agreed. "*What* does it mean? Baggage makes the dreams. People bring it in. We route it. They step off the Dreamway into a dream made from whatever they brought in. But this stuff—it doesn't have a dream destination. It's just marked Undetermined. What does that mean? Where are all of these Sleepers going?"

"So—you think this baggage is from people who are in the same place as my brother?" Stella asked.

"Possibly." Spuddle sighed. "I don't know for sure. But quite probably—wherever that is."

"Maybe there's a clue in here then," Stella said. She began to examine the objects, which were piled haphazardly, as if she were in a junkyard of valuables. A top hat, a wrench, a teapot, a bust of a raven. A notebook was half hidden beneath it, and she began to move the bust for a better look.

"Don't touch!" Spuddle screeched. He began to *click-click-click* faster than ever.

"Don't touch anything," Anyway told Stella calmly. "You'll grind the fly's gears."

"Shh!" Spuddle hushed unnecessarily. The lights went out for a long moment, then snapped on again. "Inspectors are testing the system," he whimpered. The room plunged again into darkness. "They'll reset it, and then we can duck out of here."

"What if they check this room?" Stella asked.

"They don't even know about this room!" Spuddle huffed. "This is a secret room. I only found out about it a short while ago! They'll never—"

He stopped suddenly. All three froze at the unmistakable sound of footsteps. Heavy and foreboding. And they were coming toward them.

WHERE MEMORY MEETS WATER

THE FOOTSTEPS SOUNDED THE WAY they do in movies—thudding and ominous—and drawing nearer.

Thump, thump.

"The Inspectors should stay at the conveyor belt! They shouldn't be in this area!" Spuddle whispered. "I swear, I'm going to fill out Official Complaint, Form 246A!"

"You guys seem to put a lot of faith in paperwork," Stella said.

Anyway and Spuddle stared at her in shock. "Doesn't everyone?" Spuddle asked. He hiccupped nervously.

"Look, we can discuss this later," Anyway said as

he climbed out of Stella's pocket and leaped onto a suit of armor. "But first—hide." Stella hurried to the edge of the room and pressed herself against the cold stone wall. It gave her the oddest sensation—it was as if the room had once held magic, but it had all leaked away, leaving everything deader than if it never had any in the first place.

The *clunk, clunk, clunk* of boots stopped right outside. The door rattled on its hinges. Anyway peered at Stella from the shoulder of the armor. "They won't get in," he said.

"How do you know?" Stella asked.

"I don't; I'm just saying that." Then he scurried into the visor of the armor and disappeared.

Thunk. Thunk.

She had to hide. She scanned the room for a likely place and spotted a beautifully carved chest. She didn't like the idea of being shut up inside so instead hid behind it, covering herself with a wall tapestry as the door banged on and on.

It is a horrible feeling to simply sit and wait to be

found, and Stella shivered as she shrank back against the wall.

There were a few things hidden near the chest: a silver brush, a hand mirror, and a small, oval pendant. The pendant had a symbol on the front. It was a letter A, drawn to look like a star. Stella picked up the necklace, and the moment she touched it, a feeling like a wave of electricity traveled through her.

Thunk.

She didn't know what an Inspector looked like, but if the turnstile operators were gargoyles, any horror she could imagine was possible.

She couldn't get caught.

She couldn't get kicked out of the Dreamway.

She had to find Cole. The Chimerath, or whatever it was, was sucking up his light like pasta. And it was happening fast. Stella knew it—could feel it in the real world.

She slipped the necklace into her pocket as one last, loud crash finally shattered the door. The deliberate boot steps crossed the threshold, and Stella shrank away from the sound. As she did, something small and sharp poked her in the back.

After that, everything happened at once. The tapestry she was hiding behind moved slightly; at the very same moment she realized that the thing in her back was a key—a key in a small door—and she turned it, swinging the door open. Twisting backward, she crawled into the darkness, kicking the door closed behind her. She moved forward, feeling along the wall until her fingers uncovered a hole. It seemed large enough for her. Stella squeezed her body into the hole and realized it was a pipe. She shimmied along the metal tube, forcing herself not to wonder what usually ran through it or whether or not it might start flowing at any moment. She crawled and crawled, the metal rough against her hands until—finally—a gray disk of dim light showed in the distance. A few moments longer, and she came to the end of the pipe. Her body spilled out into the semi-darkness of a large industrial area. She lowered herself on to the concrete and looked around the dark, grimy tunnel. It was a no-man's-land of steel cylinders and beams.

"Where am I now?" Stella asked out loud, and her voice echoed in the empty space.

"You're at the edge of the Memory Line," a voice replied. "Where Memory meets Water."

When Stella looked, she saw a silvery figure. She rippled like light through waves. She was a strange sort of person—small, but Stella could not tell if she was very old or very young. She had the strangest feeling that she might be both.

"You're not . . . an Inspector, are you?"

She let out a silvery laugh that almost seemed to sparkle, like light over water. "No."

"Can you help me? Do you know how can I get out of here?" Stella asked. "Is there—where can I find a door?"

The old young woman laughed again. "You don't find the doors," she said reasonably. "The doors find you."

"I—I need to get back to my friend," Stella went on. She felt the need to add, "He's a mouse."

"Is he a Door Mouse?"

"Yes."

"Then he will find you along with the door," the old young woman said. Dust motes floated and danced around the woman, shimmering like snow.

"Are you—are you a ghost? Or a memory?"

"Are those things different?"

Stella thought about this for a moment and decided that she wasn't sure.

"Do I frighten you?" The ghost began to fade, slowly, from the edges.

"No."

"Then does it matter?" She was still fading.

"I guess not. But—wait! Please don't go."

"I suggest you take a train to another station," the ghost said. "You won't find what you're looking for here."

The moment the ghost disappeared, the entire station went black. It was as if the room had dissolved and Stella was back at the beginning of time, before she—or anything—existed.

THE LIGHT AT THE END OF THE TUNNEL

Stella wasn't afraid. She was curious and confused. It was difficult to know which way to go in the total dark.

She waited a moment until, with a sudden buzz and hum, lights came on around her. These seemed to be some sort of emergency lights, and they cast a warm campfire-like glow on the walls and pipes around her. "I guess the Inspectors reset the system," she muttered to herself, and immediately regretted it, as her words echoed back to her in a way that suggested unseen things were whispering them to her on every side.

She crossed through a line of steel beams and found the tracks of what she guessed was the Memory Line.

She looked in one direction and saw nothing but orange lights stretching on into darkness. In the other, they stretched on into light. *Well,* she thought, *whatever is in that direction—at least I'll be able to see it.*

Stella started off in the direction of the light.

It took a while (How long? Who knew? In the Dreamway, time seemed to go about on its own schedule), but eventually the light grew brighter. Something gritty slid under her flip-flops, and when Stella bent to investigate, she realized that it was a layer of fine sand.

Soon, the silver rails began to gleam, and the light grew brighter.

A familiar smell wafted toward her. It took her only a moment to place it: french fries.

The sand grew deeper, and Stella stepped out from the arching tunnel and into the bright sunshine of a clear, summer day. The silver rails stretched out toward the shore and skimmed across the top of the water, disappearing into the distance.

When Stella turned back to face the way she came, she saw that she had walked out of a cave of sorts—a large triangle formed by dark boulders. Behind this and to her right was a boardwalk. She realized that this must be the source of the french fry smell. She was at a beach.

Before her was a red-and-yellow-striped beach umbrella. Underneath it was a woman in a black bathing suit and a large sunhat covering her pale complexion. A man with sable skin was building a sandcastle with a five-year-old boy with black curls. The man looked up at Stella and waved.

"Dad?" she whispered.

When the boy looked up, she saw that it was Cole. Five-year-old Cole in the navy-blue swim trunks with the whales on them. This was the summer they spent a week at the beach in New Jersey.

Stella tried to run to him, but it was hard to run in the sand, and her legs were small. When she looked down, she saw a pink bathing suit with a ruffle at the top. She hated this bathing suit. She outgrew it years ago. . . .

Is this a dream or a memory? Stella wondered. She could not feel herself walking or moving at all, but a moment later she was in the water. Cole was ahead of her, diving into the waves as they crashed toward him.

Stella remembered something—her mother had told her not to go into the water past her knees.

But Cole had gone in past his knees. He was swimming, with only his head showing above the water. She wanted to be with her brother.

Stella followed him. She shied away as a jellyfish brushed her arm. But no, she realized suddenly. It wasn't a jellyfish.

It was a piece of notebook paper.

Deep in the dream in the sea
Eyes stinging, mouth choked with salt
Overhead, the blue sky burns,
Ignores the soft white feathers of cloud.

My toes feel a swirl of sand, nothing solid, as
The waves crush forward
Something brushes my leg, wraps around my ankle,
I twist and writhe as the tentacle
Climbs my leg—the air, the air—
It's like a dream, out of reach—

BACK IN THE REAL WORLD

Gasping for air, Stella fought and clawed and, finally, drew a breath. She sat up. The light behind the curtains was gray. She was in her room again.

Relief poured through her. All she felt was gratitude, overwhelming gratitude that it had been a dream. The poem had pulled her out of sleep again, and now she was back in her world.

Her sheets were a tangled mess, so she spent a few moments arranging her bed. As she flicked the comforter into place, the calendar taped to her wall fluttered. She had forgotten to cross off yesterday, so she took the purple marker from its cup on her desk and filled the square with an X. Then she shuffled into the kitchen in her pajamas.

Tamara sat at the table, her face pale and puffy, her

hair disheveled. Cole stabbed at his breakfast cereal, his face rigid as a mask. The air in the room felt brittle, like walking into a freezer.

"What's wrong?" Stella asked.

Cole didn't look up, but her mother pulled at the chair closest to her and nodded at Stella to sit. Stella didn't move. "What's wrong?" she repeated.

"I got a communication from the unit," Tamara said gently. "They're on blackout."

Stella felt herself sway slightly; the tentacle slithered up her leg, the water pressed against her, she couldn't catch her breath. "Is he . . . dead?"

There was a moment, just half a moment, before her mother said, "No."

Cole's spoon clattered into his bowl. He put his hands over his face. Stella could hear him breathing.

The last time their father's unit went on blackout, it was because someone had been killed. The army needed time to notify the family. Stella thought about her calendar.

"He's supposed to come home in thirteen days," she whispered.

"He's fine." Her mother stood and crossed to give Stella a hug. "He's okay. It's not him." But that was horrible, too, because Stella didn't want to hope that someone else was dead. Someone else's father or mother. She didn't want that. As if she'd had the same thought, her mother said, "It could be something else entirely. We just don't know."

Cole slapped his hands against the table and stood up suddenly. "Are you okay?" Stella asked, but he didn't reply. He stood still for just a moment, then stalked out of the room.

Tamara's hazel eyes watered. "I'm sorry."

Stella knew she should say something. Something like, "It's okay," but it wasn't. Instead, she just hugged her mother.

"You don't have to go to school," Tamara offered.

"Are you staying home?"

"No, I have to go to work. I'll be home by three."

"Then I'll go to school," Stella said. Her eyes flicked to the clock. "I'd better get ready."

"Do you want something to eat on the way?" her mother asked.

"Would you toast me a bagel?"

"Sure—usual way?"

Stella hugged her mother again and went to her room to change. She took off her pajamas, and something fell out of the pocket and landed on the floor with a *clink*. It was a silver necklace. The one from the Dreamway—the one with the A formed into a star.

Stella sat down on the floor feeling as if she were an insect that had just noticed it was trapped in a jar. This necklace—it was *here*. It was *in her hand*. Up until now, there was a large piece of her—the majority, really—that had believed it was all a dream, that it truly was the same as Renee's being stuck in a giant cookie, that the real world was safe and, well, real. But now she didn't know what to think.

Is Cole literally trapped? Is that part real too? She had to talk to him.

The silver chain gleamed over her fingers as she studied the symbol again. It was never easy for her to fasten jewelry, but she had found a way to place the fastener in her rigid right hand and hold it still while she manipulated the hook in her left until it found the catch.

After several minutes, she managed to get it on. Then she pulled her shirt over it. The high crew neck covered the pendant, which grew warm against her skin.

She looked at the calendar over her bed as she dressed quickly and hurried to Cole's room, but he wasn't there. She checked the bathroom, the kitchen, the living room—he was gone. *He left without me*, she said to herself, and this was such a strange thought that she wondered for a moment if she was dreaming again. Cole never left without her, unless she was sick, and even then, he always said goodbye first.

Am I dreaming? She slapped herself across the face. It hurt the usual amount.

"I really have to stop doing that," she muttered. She didn't know what was reality anymore, and all the slapping wasn't helping.

Her gym class had moved on to running sprints, which Stella did not enjoy, but could, technically, do. So she didn't go to the library that afternoon. Instead, she and Renee trotted across the gym at what was—for Renee—a leisurely pace, which meant that she had ample oxygen to tell a long-winded story about how her mom had picked out a new couch online.

"Is—it—*pant, pant*—nice—*pant, pant*—?"

"It's boring, but nice," Renee said. "It has these cool buttons on it—"

Stella tried to pay attention to the story and to ignore the feeling of annoyance that clamped down on her chest. She was the slowest in the class, and it made her frustrated and embarrassed, even though she knew that there was no reason to be embarrassed.

A breeze blew against her neck as Cole dashed past, running into the padded mat that lined the far wall. His hair was limp against his forehead with sweat. He didn't even glance at Stella as he ran past.

"Nice running, Turbo," growled a voice as Connor sped past her.

"What did he just say to you?" Renee demanded.

"Nothing," Stella snapped. She sucked in oxygen. It was hot in the gym, and she was having trouble getting air.

Renee paused in her long-winded couch story, letting the space fill with sneaker squeaks and grunts.

"He's the worst," she said under her breath as Connor said something to Matt. They both looked at Stella and laughed.

Stella didn't reply. She focused on breathing instead.

After gym, Stella slipped back into her jeans and fresh T-shirt. Renee had dashed off to hand in a social studies paper that was late. Stella had to pass the library to get to her next class. She considered stopping in to say hello to Alice, but Ms. Slaughter was standing at the door and called, "Stella!"

"Hi."

"How are you feeling? All okay?" The librarian tilted her head slightly to look into Stella's face.

"I'm fine," she replied. She wasn't fine, of course. Her brother was disappearing, her father's unit was on blackout, and she was stuck here in the real world. But it could be worse. It could always be worse.

Ms. Slaughter looked like she was going to ask another question, but Stella couldn't bear it, so she changed the subject. "You know, I've always wondered who made that mural," she said quickly. "It's so pretty."

Ms. Slaughter looked over her shoulder at the mural

that sparkled on the wall of the library behind her desk. It was a mosaic: swirls of water edged by green shrubs beneath a silver bridge. The sky was done in shades of gray and purple, with a silver moon that gleamed in a fragment of a circle at the horizon.

"Oh." Ms. Slaughter's face clouded over. "A friend of mine made that, actually. My first year at the school, four years ago. Pedro."

Stella studied the mosaic. "Does he still make murals?"

"No, he—well, he got sick." Ms. Slaughter looked down at her desk. "Well, you'd better get going," she said quickly. "You'll be late for class."

Stella thought she saw a dark shadow pass over Ms. Slaughter's desk, but it shifted and moved toward the floor, creeping along the boards until it passed Stella's feet. The pendant at her neck felt suddenly cold, and she shuffled away to avoid the shadow.

But it had disappeared.

Or perhaps there never was a shadow at all.

Her locker was down a set of stairs and off to the right, but when she reached the landing, she saw Cole through the glass in the door. She paused with her hand on the safety bar, watching him. Connor loomed over Cole, who stared straight ahead, as if he were looking into the darkness that Stella could only sense.

"Hey, I like the way your sister runs," Connor said. "One of these days, I'll just reach out and tip her over."

Cole didn't reply.

"How'd she get so messed up?" Connor went on. "Did you drop her on her head when she was a baby, or something?"

Cole lunged at him, punching him in the stomach. Connor doubled over, and Cole cracked him again on the side of the head, and then turned. He closed his eyes for a moment, and then they snapped open. He looked directly at Stella, his eyes burning fierce and bright, like stars. And then he disappeared.

He winked out, like a candle flame, and Stella let out a scream. But in the next moment, he had reappeared. His eyes tightened into slits at her, and he stalked away.

Fear held Stella frozen in place as Connor gagged, struggling to breathe. After only a moment, she pushed open the door and asked, "Are you okay?"

"Get away from me," he snarled, still sucking in air. Straightening up, he looked after Cole, who had disappeared around a corner. "What the hell?"

"I have no idea," Stella replied.

"I'm not talking to you." Connor glared at her and walked off.

Stella stood still for a moment, overcome by thoughts of her brother.

Cole was beginning to frighten her. His strange eyes, which were alternatingly vacant pools or burning stars, his peculiar walk, which was so unlike his normal, bouncy gait, his flat voice—all of these things were evidence that he wasn't who he said he was. He was . . . vanishing. His soul really was being sucked out, *like a bowl of pasta al dente*, Anyway had said.

And the worst part, for Stella, was that the only person she wanted to talk to about all of this—was Cole.

"Is he all right?" asked a voice behind her. When Stella turned, she saw Alice.

"What?" Stella asked.

"That was your brother, right?" Alice blinked up at her. "Is he okay?"

"I don't know." Stella stared at the space where her brother had been moments before.

Alice looked thoughtful. Then she sighed and rolled off toward the cafeteria. As she passed, Stella noticed Alice's notebook tucked in its usual place, to the right of her leg. There was a symbol on the front—an A that looked like a star.

The whole of Stella's mind was occupied with Cole, though, and so she didn't wonder about that symbol, or ask herself why it was so familiar.

Later that night, Stella struggled to keep her eyes open as she worked on her homework. Dinner had been forgettable—tacos from the truck up the street. Stella loved them, but it was their standard Thursday night meal.

Cole had sat at the table, silent. Tamara didn't seem to notice his silence; she was lost in her own world too. Later, Cole had retreated to his room, where the utter quiet told Stella that he was wearing headphones or sleeping early. Stella had changed into her pajamas and settled onto her bed to read.

Stella closed her eyes for a moment, letting the poem she had just read swirl in her mind. Her homework assignment was a poem called "Ozymandias," and for some reason, the ruin in the desert had reached into her chest and squeezed her heart. She sank onto her mattress, imagining it was the "lone and level sands . . ."

"Sweetie." Tamara popped her head into Stella's room. "You need to take the trash out."

Stella's eyes snapped open, her brain taking an extra moment to reorganize and sort the world she had been reading about from the real one. The trash. Yes, that was her chore. She closed her book and placed it on her bed, then stood up. She smoothed the covers and plumped up her pillow. This was something that she and her mother had in common—when they were frightened, or sad, or confused, they became slower in their movements. Everything became deliberate. The house, strangely, became tidier, because they were living carefully, as carefully as possible.

Stella padded into the kitchen in her flip-flops and pulled the garbage from the can below the sink. A putrid smell wafted up, and she cut it off by twisting the top of the plastic bag and tying it shut. The kitchen was bright—Tamara had finally replaced the burned-out lightbulb in the under-cabinet fixture—but the surprising brilliance revealed the stain of tomato sauce on the curtains over the sink, the coffee grounds lurking in the corner, the slight rot on the banana.

Stella took the garbage and made for the hallway.

The incinerator chute was in the nook that also housed the service elevator. When they had first moved to the building, Stella had been fascinated with the idea of the chute, which had a door on every floor. The trash fell down, down into the basement, where it was delivered to the incinerator. It was satisfying to stuff it into the compartment and close the door, and then listen to the gentle scraping noises it made as it tumbled toward the basement.

Feeling as if she had at least accomplished one thing for the day, Stella turned just as the service elevator binged open.

The elevator binged again, and the door began to close, but Stella lunged forward and thrust her arm between the door and the wall. It hit her wrist and stopped, then rolled back open. She stepped inside.

The door paused, open, as if asking if she was sure she wanted to stay. Then it rolled deliberately shut. A light blinked on. SSB the button read. Sub-Subbasement. Stella had never noticed that button before. The elevator descended slowly, picking up speed as it traveled down from 3 to 2 to G to B. It fell faster as it passed the Sub-basement, then faster still, and faster, until Stella was dizzy with the swaying box. She felt like the garbage, tumbling downward into unknown space.

She was frightened. She pushed the emergency stop button, but the elevator did not stop. It fell and fell until, finally, abruptly, it *halted*. It didn't crash. It stopped with a yank, then gently fell a bit farther as if to settle itself.

She pressed against the back wall as the door rattled open, revealing a ruin. Tall, half-crumbled columns stood beneath the open sky, like a forest that had survived a fire or flood. The floors were white marble. Overhead, the many stars were set with pointillistic illustrations of unfamiliar constellations. Unlike constellations in our world, these were easy to see. One was a mighty woman with wings driving a chariot. Another showed a large butterfly. It was a sky unlike anything Stella had seen in real life—it was a sky like an illustration in a book.

A station, she thought. *I'm in a train station.*

At the center of the station was a tall four-sided clock with both hands at twelve. Here and there, Sleepers bustled silently through the ruin. Stella wasn't sure where to go, until she spotted an information booth. Just before she reached it, she caught a movement out of the corner of her eye. Something was streaking toward her—it was Anyway, and he was shouting something, but his tiny voice couldn't carry far.

Stella raced toward him, and in a few steps, she heard him shout, "No! No! The other way!" It was then that she noticed his wide eyes, the panic in his voice—and the machine behind him.

It was all arms, all legs, like a spider made of pipes, and as it crashed across the station, everything—the constellations, the columns, the marble floor—everything shuddered and vibrated. Anyway was at the edge of it, staying inches ahead with every desperate step.

Stella stopped so suddenly that she slid, fell, and had to pull herself up again, scrambling to her feet. She and Anyway raced toward the elevator that she had just exited.

She could hear the tiny puffs of his breathing, felt the strain in her chest as she ran, trying to outpace this monstrosity.

"Don't let it grab you!" Anyway shouted. "It's an Inspector!"

DEAD MILEAGE

STELLA AND ANYWAY RACED TOWARD the elevator, but the door was shut. She wanted to cry out, but she had no air. The distance between her and the elevator was closing, but so was the distance between her and the Inspector.

"Here! Over here!" A buzzing sound whirred toward them, and Anyway darted to the left. Stella was about to shout, "No, that's the wrong way!" when she saw a golden flash in the air and realized that Spuddle was screeching, "Over here! Over here!" and turning small flips in the air.

Stella forced her legs to follow him, and the clockwork dragonfly hurtled toward an archway. *A train*, Stella thought. *We'll catch a train!* But when they raced through the arch, the tracks were empty.

"This way!" Spuddle cried, zipping across the rails and then diving to the ground before disappearing completely.

"Don't touch the third rail," Anyway warned as Stella jumped down onto the tracks.

"I know." She picked up the mouse and placed him in her pocket. At the center of the tracks was an open manhole. Spuddle popped up out and said, "This is it!" before disappearing again.

Stella looked at the hole. It was black, as frightening as the thing that was coming after them. But she forced herself to think of Spuddle, a bright glimmer in the dark, as she placed her legs at the edge of the hole and dropped inside.

She landed with a splash, but the water was only a thin puddle. Light trickled in from the manhole.

"Look," Anyway whispered. She titled her head upward. As she watched, the metal thing stormed past, sending chunks of marble flying. From his place inside her pocket, Anyway's tiny mouse heart whirred against hers at a rate of 500 beats per minute.

A spark flared, and Spuddle appeared. A small candle flame burned from his tail. It was barely enough to see by—it illuminated no more than two feet ahead of him, which wasn't enough to reach the floor or the walls. But it was enough to see each others' faces.

"What was that?" Stella asked.

"Ehrm," Anyway said awkwardly. "Well, you see, I had to do a little unauthorized door-switching to find you again. . . ."

"The Inspectors didn't like it much," Spuddle volunteered.

Stella shuddered. "They're worse than I imagined," she admitted.

"I should hope so," Spuddle replied. "Who would imagine those things?"

Stella turned to Spuddle. "So—where are we going?"

"To see Dr. Peavey, of course," Spuddle replied. "To find out where Cole is."

"I meant—which direction?" Stella explained.

He blinked at her brightly, causing the light to flicker. "I'm so glad you asked!" He blinked again, and then let out a little cough.

"Well . . . what's the answer?" Stella asked.

"I don't know," Spuddle admitted. "Anyway?"

The Door Mouse sighed. "Forward," he snapped.

"Excellent plan!" Spuddle congratulated him.

And so they went forward through the darkness with only a dim light to see by. Stella flinched and let out a small cry. "Something slithered across my foot!" She shook her leg, and her flip-flop flapped against her heel.

"Oh, that's just a little bugaboo," Anyway replied. "Try not to touch the walls—they can be *very* worrisome."

They walked in silence. Stopping suddenly, Stella asked, "Did you hear that?"

Spuddle paused in the air. "I don't hear anything."

"What was it?" Anyway asked, his voice suspicious.

Every now and again, when Spuddle drifted close to one of the walls, Stella would catch sight of a complex web of cables and ducts. She would also catch *movement*—things crawling and wriggling along the pipes. She shuddered.

Time is a very difficult thing to have a sense of

when you are walking along in the dark. Time didn't make much sense in the Dreamway as it was, but inside this strange tunnel, alive with pipes and creatures, time almost ceased to exist. There was only this, only now.

They had been walking. They were walking. They would be walking. The future was something best left alone.

Stella stumbled, pitching sideways. She windmilled her arms to balance herself and fell against the wall. An insect scurried across her hand, traveling up her arm.

"Ouch!" It had bitten her. She shook it off, but the bite made her arm feel as if it was on fire. She stumbled again.

"Stop!" Anyway shouted as Spuddle cried, "What is it?"

But Stella didn't answer. The darkness was parting. Ahead, there was a light. The light grew brighter and brighter, until the brilliance was as blinding as the dark had been. More than blinding—it was a white like the fire on her body, and she felt as if she were a flame, burning, burning away. . . .

She stood alone at the center of a stone labyrinth,

wondering, Which way? Which way? *In every direction, an identical opening. She took a step toward one, and then hesitated.*

Maybe it doesn't matter, *she thought. Just as she was about to take another step, someone called her name.*

She froze. Every hair on her body stood on end. It was Cole.

"Stella!" he cried.

Behind her.

Turning, she plunged into the gap between boulders, Overhead, the sun burned as she raced toward Cole's voice. It was hot. The stone beneath her feet radiated through her flip-flops.

"Stella!"

It was to her left. She doubled back, racing toward the voice. Could she get to her brother? The stone walls rose above the crown of her head but cast no shadows.

"Stella!"

Forward, forward, and suddenly, she was out of it. The labyrinth was behind her, and before her stretched a vast ocean of sand, and nothing more.

BITTEN

HER THROAT BURNED; SHE WAS SO thirsty.

"Stella!" someone hissed. "Stella!" Needles scratched at her neck.

Stella's eyelids were heavy; they opened slowly, then closed again as a light flashed into them.

"Stella, wake up!" Anyway scratched at her neck again with his sharp little claws. "Wake up!"

"Wake up! Wake up!" Spuddle's high-pitched voice sounded like a shriek, even when he wasn't panicked, as he was now.

Stella opened her eyes and managed to focus. "I'm . . . thirsty . . ." she croaked.

"We'll get you water," Anyway promised. "But you have to go farther. Can you stand up?"

Stella wobbled to her feet, careful to avoid touching the walls. She wiped her hands on her pajama top and brushed her hair out of her eyes. As she stood in a puddle of light, surrounded by darkness, she felt her heart sink. "How much farther?" she whispered.

"Not much," Anyway said, and Stella decided to believe him.

"What happened?" Stella asked.

"A bugaboo bit you." Anyway explained. He gestured contemptuously toward the crawlies on the wall. "It must have been a big one—I've never seen anyone get so sick."

"Come, come!" Spuddle cried. "Hurry! And don't touch the walls."

Stella concentrated on putting one foot in front of the other. Her arm throbbed; her throat burned. She had to move. She had to keep moving. The idea of getting stuck in this dark tunnel, the way she had been stuck in the labyrinth, of never getting out, that was something that she tried to keep at the edges of her mind. She didn't want to look at it closely; it was too terrifying.

But it turned out that Anyway had been telling the truth after all. It wasn't long before they saw something ahead. It wasn't exactly a light; it was more like the end of the darkness. A patch of gray beckoned toward them, and Stella kept moving.

Spuddle raced ahead.

"Get back here, you dumb fly!" Anyway shouted. "We can't see a thing!"

The dragonfly buzzed back, mumbling sorry, and had to content himself with doing nervous little flips in the air.

Finally, they came to the end and could see out into the gray. Steel beams and pylons decorated in a tangled mass of graffiti stood before them. Everything—even the ceiling—was painted in a colorful jumble and covered in a layer of dirt and grime. Low fluorescent lights buzzed and flickered here and there along the ceiling.

"Is it—is it a station?" Stella asked.

"Dead Mileage," Anyway told her. "Nonoperational track."

"Trains haven't come here in centuries," Spuddle agreed.

"But someone has," Stella noted, looking at the graffiti.

"*The Pirate*," Anway said darkly. "Dead Mileage belongs to the Pirate. The good news is that if we cut through here, we can get to the Nightmare Line faster. I think," he added under his breath.

At the end of the duct, there was a drop of six feet to the track. Stella's body blazed with pain as she landed on her feet, and she shuddered. The hallucination still clung to her like a spiderweb.

"Are you okay?" Anway asked.

She sucked in a breath, then another. "Yes," she hissed finally. She put her hands on her knees to help bring herself upright, but the pressure made her gasp.

"What is it? What is it?" Spuddle demanded.

"It's just—my arm," Stella explained. She pulled back her sleeve. The two puncture wounds oozed dark purple in the dim light, and her wrist was swollen.

"Bring it closer," Anway growled.

Stella held her arm near the mouse, so he could look at it. "Why is this happening?" she demanded. "This place isn't even real—it's all just . . ." she hissed an angry sigh. "My arm was *fine*," she whispered to herself.

Anyway didn't answer. He leaned forward, sniffing it, then recoiled. He looked up at Stella, his face a mix of rage and worry. "Let's keep moving." Anyway commanded, and—since they had no choice—they obeyed.

She reached for Anyway with her good hand and placed him back into her pocket. She was, after all, used to mostly using one arm. Then the friends made their way to the tracks. The platform came almost to Stella's head, and even the space from the platform to the track was covered in paint. As they walked along the track, Stella inspected the graffiti. Some of it was beautiful—words like *Hope* and *Faith* painted in brilliant, interlocking letters. Every now and again, they would hear a soft noise, and the three would stop. But, always, after a moment all would be still, and they would move on.

"What—what does the Pirate—do?" Stella asked.

"Same as all Pirates," Anyway grumbled. "Steals things, moves on."

"He doesn't follow the *rules*!" Spuddle said fiercely. "You can't just take things in and out of the Dreamway!"

Stella blinked slowly, and then nodded. She forced herself to pay attention, to stay awake. It was difficult, though. Her brain felt as if it were made of wads of dense felt placed at the bottom of a murky well. Things were having trouble moving through it and traveling to her furry tongue. It was as if her synapses—instead of forming quick connections—had all decided to go for a long solitary walk in separate dark forests. "Is the Pirate with . . . the Inspectors?"

Anyway gave a little mouse snort. "No."

Stella nodded, but talking was becoming more difficult for her. She was a flashlight with a weak battery.

And then she heard it—her name. Without thinking, she stopped and shouted, "Cole?"

Spuddle hushed her loudly, and Anyway said, "Do you want to get us killed?"

But she heard it, like an echo of the hallucination— it *was* Cole; he was calling her. She stumbled forward, trying to run, but her feet were clumsy, her arm stiff

178

and throbbing, like too much sausage about to split the casing.

"Stop!" Anyway shouted, but she was staggering forward, toward the voice. "Stop! Stop!"

Crash.

This noise stopped them in their tracks.

"What was that?" Spuddle whispered.

Stella swayed on her feet, then sat down hard on the filthy tracks. Her eyes closed, then snapped open, then closed again.

"Oh, no," Anyway said with a gasp. "Stella?"

She let out a groan. Anyway crept from her pocket and looked at her arm. It was a furious red; the bugaboo's poison had gone deep.

Pounding foosteps echoed behind them.

"Is it—?" Spuddle asked.

"Not sure," Anyway replied. "But no matter what, it's not something we want to find us."

Spuddle *tick*ed and *sproing*ed. "Oh, I shall file such a report! I'll write a letter the likes of which have never been *imagined*—" His words ended in a scream as a figure raced toward them. Spuddle darted backward, but the figure reached out and plucked him from the air. The face remained in shadow as thick, strong fingers held the fly up to dark eyes.

"Well, what do we have here?" asked the Pirate.

THE PIRATE

IT WAS A SLOW, UNCERTAIN journey through the Dead Mileage, and Anyway spent the entire time berating himself for his lack of courage. He called himself miserable, wretched, useless, pathetic—enough words to make a thesaurus proud. "I know right from wrong," Anyway griped. "And sometimes, I even care about the difference! Oh, why didn't I put up a fight?"

"What happened to her?" the Pirate asked, eyeing Stella.

"Bitten by the worry bug," Anyway said. "A bugaboo."

Spuddle squeaked. "This section of track has not been properly maintained—"

"Of course not. Nobody here but me." The Pirate

inspected Stella's arm and then looked at her carefully. "How did she get in?" The Pirate's voice was sharp. He pulled something from his pocket.

"Don't touch her," Anyway snarled as the Pirate leaned toward Stella. "I'll bite your finger!"

The Pirate looked at him a moment with steady black eyes. He wore a leather cap with earflaps, a pair of goggles perched atop his head. "She's sick," the Pirate said. "She needs a small dose of Reality." He held out a bottle. "I'll cure her fears, but—it will take a while." The Pirate pulled a cork from the bottle and held it toward Stella's lips, but Anyway lunged at it, blocking the way.

"How do I know you're not going to poison her?" Anyway demanded.

The Pirate chuckled softly. "You don't have much of a choice, Door Mouse. But I don't kill people," the Pirate said. "Besides, I know her. That's Stella Clay."

BITTER TRUTH

"Stella. Stella!"

Stella forced open her eyes and found herself staring into a familiar face. *This* was the Pirate? He was her age. How could that be?

"Just another drop," the Pirate said, placing something to her lips.

"Ugh." Stella screwed up her mouth. "It's awful."

"The bitter truth." The Pirate didn't smile, but his eyes laughed. "Cuts through worry, even if it's unpleasant."

"You don't have to drink any more of it," Anyway said. He was perched on Stella's knee, watching her closely. "Just a taste is enough."

With a sigh, Stella closed her eyes and leaned back.

Then she opened them again. Her head was clearing slowly, like fog burning off as the sun comes out. The Pirate studied her face for a moment, and then stood up. He was tall and slender, surprisingly graceful.

"I have something for you," he announced. He walked over to a leather bag, where he rummaged around for a few moments, finally pulling out a worn and tattered notebook. "Here," he said, handing it to her.

Stella looked at it for a moment, then flipped through the pages. It was her brother's. The rest of it, whole and intact.

Deep in the dream in the desert
Still burning underneath the desert sun,
I know that I have dreamed this place before
This is my father's desert—it's the one
I see when I imagine him at war.

I turn to run as a tank rolls toward me.
Beneath my feet, I hear the metal catch
Of a land mine

If I step off,
It will explode.

The tank . . .
It's coming for me, and . . .
I . . .
Can't . . .
Move. . . .

She held the papers in her hand and felt herself pulled in two directions, both downward and upward—the ground collapsed, sand pouring into a pit, and it sucked at her legs like a living thing. Above her, the clouds parted and the sky pulled with searing intensity, and both the sky and the earth reverberated with her name. Cole was calling from above, from below—her heart raced, her throat closed, her head felt light, and the pain of being pulled in two directions made her think she might be split in half when the sky went suddenly white—

And she was back in the Dreamway.

Cole's poem had almost pulled her back into her

world, but something had kept her here. She looked at the notebook and then glanced at the Pirate. "Where did you get this?"

"I found it." The Pirate removed his aviator's cap and ran a hand over his short, spiky black hair. "I knew who it belonged to."

"How did you know who it belonged to?" Anyway demanded, looking closely at the paper.

The Pirate smiled. "Ask Stella."

Stella was about to say no, don't ask her, because she had no idea. But those eyes . . . the face was so familiar. . . .

And then she had it.

"Alice?" she said, her voice a whisper.

"Fancy meeting you here." And now it was obvious. Alice Yun was here in the Dreamway.

"You two know each other?" Anyway asked. He gaped at Alice. "And wait—I thought you were a boy! Girls can't be pirates!"

"Tell that to Mary Wolverston," Alice snapped.

Anyway sniffed. "I don't know her."

"Obviously not," Alice replied. "Because she was a pirate."

Stella sat up straighter. "How did you get here?"

"I could ask you the same question."

"I—I just—I don't really know."

Alice sat down on the floor and folded her long legs beneath her. "Interesting."

"Do *you* know?"

"I've been able to get here for . . . years," Alice admitted. "Ever since the accident, actually."

"You can't have," Anyway huffed.

Alice shrugged. "Okay," she said.

Stella looked at her. "You're different." She didn't want to say, "You're not in your wheelchair," but Alice knew what she meant.

"When I was in the hospital, I used to dream that I could still walk. Still dance. In my dreams, nothing had changed."

Stella thought about her own right hand and leg and how easily they moved in the Dreamway. "Yes."

"I liked dreaming. So I worked on it until I was good

at it. I found I could come here whenever I wanted, but I could only stay a little while. I'd always hit an exit in my dreams. But then I started *really* working at it—I'd sort of *wake up* in my dreams, and then I'd concentrate. I'd look for the exits and I'd just avoid them. After a while, I could stay longer and longer until eventually, one night—I wandered out of my dream onto the tracks. And now I come here when I want some alone time, and when I want to paint. In the real world—"

"The Penumbra," Anyway corrected.

"Whatever—I live with my dad. I love him, but . . ."

"Is that how you started—taking stuff?" Stella asked.

"I only take things from the Dross," Alice replied.

"What's that?"

"The leavings," Spuddle explained. "The very end of a dream. What's left over once a Sleeper exits a dream."

"I filch it before it gets recycled. It's just junk, anyway. But some of the stuff in the storage area is really interesting." Stella thought of the hideous Barney lamp. "It makes you wonder about people."

"But—you never answered my question," Stella

prompted. "Why do you come here?"

"I like moving around on my own, you know? Seeing things. My dad—he doesn't like to let me out of his sight. Here, I'm free. So—now you answer my question. What are *you* doing here?"

Quickly, Stella explained how Cole had been kidnapped by a Chimerath, how he was somewhere in the Dreamway. "His paper was marked Undisclosed."

"I'm hoping Dr. Peavey can tell us where he is," Anyway filled in. "Somewhere on the Nightmare Line."

"Weird," Alice said. She glanced at the notebook in Stella's hands. "So—you think the Chimerath is *dragging* him through the Dreamway?"

Stella nodded. "And I think . . . I think he's dropping scraps of paper—like Hansel and Gretel. To lead me to him."

"Undisclosed," Alice said slowly, thinking.

"Yes, it's . . . peculiar," Spuddle chimed in, in a voice that suggested it was more than peculiar, that in fact nefarious was the better word, but he was too delicate to suggest such a thing.

"Strange doings along the Nightmare Line," Alice said.

"What do you mean?" Anyway asked sharply.

"Look at your map."

The mouse pulled it out from the pouch around his neck. Alice took it from him as it grew, unfolding to the size of a diner menu. Stella stared at it. It was interesting to watch as the map flickered and changed. She noticed that the tracks did seem to stay relatively in the same place, but the station names shifted and changed, and sometimes one would disappear or another new one pop up from nowhere. The Nightmare Line existed mostly independently, intersecting with only a few other lines—Memory, Metaphor, Water, and Daily Life. But now the Nightmare Line flickered on the map, at times blinking more brightly than all the other lines combined.

"I've heard noises," Alice said. "Something is happening there."

Anyway and Stella exchanged a glance. "Curiouser and curiouser," Anyway said.

"I think it should be 'more and more curious,'"

Stella replied. She was a firm supporter of standard grammar.

"Curiosity killed the cat," Spuddle put in ominously.

"Well, then, it's lucky that I'm a mouse," Anyway replied.

After a moment, Alice turned to Stella. "How's the arm?"

Stella looked down. "It doesn't hurt anymore. It's like it wasn't even real." She thought for a moment. "Maybe it wasn't."

Alice pressed her lips together, considering. "Back in our world," she began, "I can't feel my legs, you know? If you touch them, I don't feel it. But every now and then, I get these pains. Pains in legs that can't feel anything."

"So—is that real?"

"I guess that kind of question just doesn't help much," Alice said slowly. "It might not be 'real,' but it really hurts. So I just tell myself this kind of pain can't kill me, and that's how I get through it." She studied Stella's face. If she was suggesting something, Stella couldn't figure out what it was. Then Alice turned to the mouse. "You'd better stop door-switching, you know. You're not a Door Mouse anymore."

"One does not simply stop being a Door Mouse," Anyway huffed.

"You're not a Door Mouse anymore?" Stella asked. "You never mentioned that."

"Peavey fired all the Door Mice. He just announced a major restructuring." Alice laughed, but it wasn't a pretty sound. "He said it would 'do wonders for the economy, offering exciting opportunities for those willing to help grow the job market in cutting-edge new industries.'"

Stella's jaw dropped. "Is that how this place works?" she asked.

"It's not how anyplace works," Alice shot back. "But *definitely* not here."

"I suspect," Spuddle interjected, "that this all comes back to someone misfiling the appropriate paperwork."

"Oh, it's misfiled all right," Alice said.

"Curiouser and curiouser," Anyway repeated. "And curiouser," he added.

Alice sighed.

"But who is Peavey?" Stella demanded. "Why does he get to fire people?"

"He's the one who sorted out the Dreamway when it got too chaotic," Anyway answered. "All the baggage was getting mixed up, so he organized the lines and came up with the baggage system."

"It seems pretty clear," Alice said, "that whatever is going on, Peavey is the one with the answers."

"We've got to get to him ASAP," Stella agreed.

"What does that mean?" Anyway asked suspiciously.

"All Sesquipedalian Anteaters Preen," Spuddle explained.

"What does sesquipedalian mean?" Anyway asked.

"Six-footed," Spuddle told him. "Obviously."

"I know a shortcut," said Alice, who was—very wisely—ignoring the whole exchange. "But I don't think you'll like it."

THE SHORTCUT

STELLA FELT BETTER AS ALICE led them through the twists and turns of the nonoperational track. Her arm still throbbed, but it didn't burn. Her mind still retained wisps of cloud, but every movement made it feel clearer.

Although they were not exactly close friends, finding Alice in the Dreamway had made Stella feel more confident. Alice knew the Dreamway, at least this section of it. Anyway rode along in a dark silence, but Spuddle buzzed in excited circles around Alice's head.

"I can't believe your collection!" Spuddle gushed to Alice. "It's wonderful! And to think that all of this came from Dross! No one ever complained that it wasn't returned. I'll have to alert the offi—"

"No," Alice said.

"Why not?"

"I don't put as much faith in bureaucracy as you do."

Spuddle stopped up short in midair. "I . . . don't . . ." He clanged and pinged, as if someone had wound him too tightly.

The Dead Mileage was an interesting section, in the creepy way that old abandoned warehouses can be interesting. In one part, someone had discarded a group of perhaps thirty mannequins. Several were headless, armless, or legless, and separated limbs littered the floor. The scene reminded Stella of one of her fairy tales, "The White Cat," and sent a shiver across her scalp. At another point, there were several abandoned subway cars. One had a family of possums living inside, but they hid when they saw the group coming along.

Once, Alice stopped and seemed to reconsider. Then she turned around.

"Are we lost?" Stella asked her.

"Thought I heard something," Alice replied. "New direction."

It was interesting how Stella's eyes had grown

accustomed to the dim light. Or perhaps this was just a function of the Dreamway—her senses were heightened, and she knew things were there even when she couldn't see them. Pipes and ducts ran along the curved tunnel ceiling, but there was space here. They could walk easily, and every step created an echo.

"Do you hear that?" Stella asked, pausing a moment.

Alice stopped, too, and gestured to Spuddle to be still. The dragonfly landed on a pylon and perched quietly. Anyway snapped out of his sullen silence to peek from Stella's pocket. The silence stretched in every direction as they strained to hear. Alice was just about to give up when they all heard it—a steady thrum, like the rhythm of a jackhammer. It reverberated for a moment and then stopped.

"What is it?" Stella asked. She did not mention that she had heard something else—Cole's voice mixed in with the jackhammer.

"Track maintenance," Anyway said.

"Maintenance on nonoperational track?" Alice asked. "It doesn't make sense."

"What's that?" Spuddle gestured toward a patch of

light to the right of them. They raced down a long tunnel that ended suddenly and stepped out into gray mist. Not far away was the lacework of a suspension bridge.

"So—where, exactly, does this go?" Stella asked as the friends hurried toward the bridge. Thick mist licked at them, and Stella thought that it looked as if they were about to plunge into a cloud. She was a few steps ahead, and a fleecy vapor cast a veil over her, hiding her from view. Alice turned to answer. But she didn't answer. Instead, when the vapor passed away, Alice had disappeared. "Alice?" Stella cried.

"Pirate!" Spuddle shouted.

Stella darted forward, missed her footing, and plunged (farther and longer than she had expected) down into the mysterious gray.

WHAT

Landing on her side, Stella slipped round and round and down, twirling like a corkscrew. "Anyway?" she shouted, pinwheeling her arms into the thick stew of mist.

"It's a slide!" Anyway shouted from her pocket. "I hate slides!" He let out a squeaking screech.

Stella stuck out her legs, trying to arrest her fall, but she plunged faster, farther.

"I'm coming!" shrieked Spuddle's voice above them.

Stella landed in a snowbank with a sudden *plomp*. She wasn't hurt. She wasn't even cold, she realized as she sat up.

"I think I'm going to be sick," Anyway said.

"Not in my pocket, you're not," Stella told him.

Snow fell from a gray sky, blowing against a visible gust across the path before them. The edges of the snowy walkway were lined with birches—slender trees with papery white bark. Stella had seen snow many times, but she was used to a greater contrast—black branches and streetlamps, dirt and grime mixed in with the snow. Here, everything was white on white, with the exception of the dark, slender markings on the trunks of the birches. Stella did what she always did in an unexpected snow—she held back her head and stuck out her tongue, where a flake landed lightly and stubbornly refused to melt. In fact, it got stuck at the back of her throat.

She fished it out with a finger and inspected it.

A mound of snow shuddered nearby, and then a head popped out. It was Alice, who snorted little flakes out of her nose and hacked a few times.

Anyway studied the sky. "What is it?" he asked.

Alice held up a handful. "It's . . . paper," she said.

Reaching out with his paw, Anyway caught a falling flake and inspected it closely. He let out a sudden gasp. "It's not just paper. It's . . . *paperwork*!"

It was Spuddle's turn to gasp as Anyway looked

around. "I suppose that's what happens when you have to fill out everything in octuplicate," the mouse said.

"That's what happens . . ." Alice said slowly, ". . . when you *shred* everything in octuplicate."

Spuddle screeched, "They shredded it!?" Frantically, he zipped from one fragment to the next, trying to put them back together. After a few moments, it became clear that the task was impossible and he burst into tears. "All my work! They shredded it all!"

Awkwardly, Stella hauled herself to her feet. After helping Alice out of the paper bank, Stella stared around at the landscape. The white falling from the sky was, in fact, confetti—huge drifts of it had gathered at the edges of the path and at the roots of the birches. When she stepped closer, she realized that the birches, too, were not trees. Stella reached out to touch one. Peering closer, she read the words. It looked like a page from her mother's economics textbook.

It was slightly easier to slog through paper shreds than snow but made more annoying by the fact that little pieces kept sticking to Stella's wool sweater.

"It's only a bit farther," Anyway said as Stella

shuffled her feet through the shreds.

After a while, they came to a clearing, at the center of which was an enormous white desk. Suspended from an overhanging branch was a black-and-white television set. "An orderly Dreamway is a happy Dreamway," the image of Dr. Peavey said. "Which is why all forms must be filled out in octuplicate and given to the Management Office, where they can be properly filed and processed. . . ." It blared on and on. On the other side of the desk was a door.

"Can I help you?" asked a voice, and that was when Stella noticed the frog sitting on a corner of the desk, half-hidden by a pile of papers.

"*What!*" Anyway spat, and Spuddle gasped.

"What?" Stella asked.

"Yes." Anyway peered up at her. "Him. That's What."

"What's what?" Stella repeated.

"I'm going to just assume that this makes sense to you all," Alice told them.

"Please allow me to cut this short," said the frog. "My name is What, and I am the Under Secretary in

Charge of Paperwork. Hello . . . *Anyway*."

"We're here to see Peavey," Anyway replied.

"Let's see . . ." The frog flipped languidly through an appointment book. "Do you have an appointment?"

"You know very well that we don't," Anyway snapped.

"Well, I'm afraid that Dr. Peavey isn't available," What replied cheerfully. He flipped several pages in his book. "Ah! Here we go. How about next Tuesday at nine a.m.? Would that be convenient?"

"That will *not* be convenient!" Spuddle shouted, ticking and springing with rage. "Just as it would not be convenient to file form after form and wait patiently for replies that never come only to realize that my forms have been shredded to bits!"

"Are you sure you filed them properly?" What challenged.

Spuddle's eyes grew enormous with fury. "How dare you imply that I can't file a simple form in octuplicate! Filing forms in octuplicate has been *my life's work*!" The dragonfly's outrage flared so hot that Stella momentarily feared he might set fire to the whole forest. "And even if it wasn't filed properly, I'd like to know why I haven't been notified of its progress!" His voice reached a hysterical pitch and, suddenly, his ticking reminded Stella of a time bomb.

"Now, really, my dear dragonfly—"

Stella felt time pressing on her shoulders. Cole was out there—somewhere. Who knew how long it would be before he disappeared forever? Anyway had said it could happen in as little as a few days. This was the third day, and Cole was definitely slipping away. She slammed her hand on the desk and everyone jumped.

"I have to talk to Dr. Peavey," Stella said. "Now."

What cleared his throat. "I just told you that the earliest I can get you in is—excuse me, where do you think you're going? Don't touch that! Don't you dare open that!" The frog shrieked as Stella walked past his desk and reached for the doorknob.

"Don't move," What commanded. "Nobody move! Don't you dare go in there—"

"We are *definitely* going in there," Anyway snapped.

"I am calling security—"

"Don't twitch a single slimy webbed finger,"

Spuddle warned, flicking open the flame on his tail. "If you do, I'll burn this place down."

"You wouldn't dare!" What shot back.

"All my life . . ." Spuddle's voice was a low grumble and buzz. "All my life, I have filed the proper paperwork. I have filled it out according to directions. I have sent it in and waited carefully for a reply. And when a reply never came, I waited some more. I maintained faith. I *believed*. And now—" He looked around at the drifts of shredded paper. "Now . . . I see that my faith was pointless." His voice dropped to a hiss. "Pointless. So don't tell me that I won't burn it down. It's already burned down. *You burned it down!*" Spuddle quivered with rage and the flame on his tail flared.

What stood there, his mouth agape. For a frog who was surrounded by words, he didn't have anything to say. Everyone else exchanged glances for a moment, until finally Stella said, "So—uh—I suppose I'll just go ahead?"

Nobody tried to stop her.

"Spuddle—better put that away," Stella said, gesturing to the flame.

"We'll see." He continued his crazy-eyed stare at What.

Stella stepped through the door and found herself in a room about the size of her bedroom. It was brilliant with lights, and a camera was set up, pointed at Dr. Peavey, who continued to announce Dreamway policies as if she hadn't walked in there. Her friends followed her inside.

"Excuse me, sir," Spuddle clicked off his lighter and flew over to him, "but I have repeatedly filed Form 329 B—"

Dr. Peavey droned on.

"Excuse me," Spuddle repeated, but Dr. Peavey ignored him. "I think I deserve your attention!" the dragonfly said. He zoomed past the doctor's head, brushing past his toupee.

Dr. Peavey's head fell off.

Spuddle screamed.

"You've killed him!" Anyway shouted.

Unconcerned, Dr. Peavey continued to deliver his message as Alice and Stella gaped at each other. Stella bent over him, but the minute she touched his chest, a black shadow vomited from his mouth and poured out the door.

"He's a puppet!" Anyway screeched. "What!" He leaped out of Stella's pocket, landing with an awkward tumble. Recovering quickly, the mouse scampered through the door, where the frog was shoving things into a tiny briefcase. The moment he saw Anyway, What let out a croak and hopped from the desk. The mouse scurried after him, and a hopping-flopping-skittering-scrambling chase ensued. "We need answers, you amphibious *coward*!"

"He's making for the door!" Spuddle screeched, and Stella saw what he meant—one of the trees nearby had a doorknob in the trunk. What yanked it open and tried to jerk it closed behind him, but Spuddle swooped into the crack. The door closed on him with a clatter and clink.

"Spuddle!" Anyway cried, racing to his friend's side. Stella reached him at the same moment while Spuddle dove after What.

"Ow! Stop that!" What cried as Spuddle punched at his head. "Stop it!"

"Spuddle!" Anyway wailed.

The dragonfly stopped and turned to face Anyway. "I'm fi—" he began, but his voice died in his throat. Stella and Anyway followed his gaze. They were still outside the tree, and this was the first time that they had really noticed the room that What had tried to escape into. The door was the width of the tree, which was only just wide enough for Stella to squeeze inside. But the room extended far beyond the trunk. It was the size of a warehouse and packed floor to ceiling with stuff. Everything from stuffed animals to lampshades, matador capes to flying trapezes, a marble fountain that looked like a gargling fish, an entire pirate ship—a million and one things piled and jumbled, like a city dump.

"Baggage," Alice said as she joined them. "More than I've ever seen!"

"The *missing* baggage," Spuddle whispered. "The *light* baggage, the positive charges—" Giving himself a rattling shake, he lunged at What again. "What is the meaning of this?!" screeched the little dragonfly. "Why has this baggage been diverted?"

"People don't need this stuff!" What insisted.

"Of course they need it," Stella said. "Of *course*." She thought of Cole's notebook.

"No they don't." What's voice was a sneer. "When we made dreams from positive charges, what happened? Used to be that people would *listen*. People would get *inspired*. But that stopped working, didn't it? People ignored the positive dreams and only listened to the negative ones. And why is that? Because people don't want to be *inspired*—they want to be *frightened*. They don't do anything unless they're scared. Not anymore."

"That's not true!" Stella insisted.

"Isn't it?" The frog frowned at her. "People *need* Nightmares."

"You made a deal with them, didn't you?" Anyway demanded. "The Chimerath. You're the reason this is happening. You're the reason Dr. Peavey is . . . like that."

"Hah! He had risen to his level of incompetence," What said. "What a slob. I worked with him for centuries, so I know! He was fine when he was in charge of the Reality Line. But managing the *whole system*?"

"Who put him in charge?"

"He did! He installed himself here and said light dreams and dark dreams wouldn't get mixed up anymore. He'd make sure that the lines were run separately. Separately but equal!"

"That never works," Stella pointed out.

"Of course it doesn't," What snapped. "Believe me, I pointed it out many times, but did he listen? No! Slowly, but surely, the Chimerath grew stronger. And when they came for him, there was nothing I could do! I didn't want anyone to know, so I just made a puppet. Plenty of materials for papier-mâché around here."

"You didn't tell anyone." Spuddle's voice was flat. "You just . . . let the Chimerath have him."

"Oh, like *you* would have stood up to them," What sneered.

Spuddle blinked. "I might be afraid of things," he said simply, "but I'm not a coward. I'm not a liar. I'm not a"—he looked around at the tiny paper scraps that covered everything—"a *shredder*."

"What's this?" Alice asked suddenly, plucking a half-folded paper that hung out of the frog's hastily packed briefcase.

"Give that back!" What cried, but Alice was already unfolding it, asking, "What are you trying to hide, there, frog?" She studied the paper, her face growing very serious.

"What is it?" Stella asked.

Alice looked up. Her face was pale and her mouth hung open, as if she couldn't find the words for what she wanted to say. She turned the paper around.

"It's a . . . map," Anyway said slowly.

"Do you see?" Alice said, pointing to a fat line that ran almost entirely across the page. Even as the other lines shifted and changed, this one remained a permanent dark scar.

"What's that?" Spuddle demanded. "That's not any line I know."

"It's *new*," What said, and his mouth pursed up into a little button.

"A *new* Nightmare Line," Anyway said.

"It cuts across everything!" Spuddle cried. Spuddle let out a horrified gasp and gaped at Stella. "Everything!"

"Is that a problem?" Stella asked.

"Yes, that is a terrible problem," Anyway snapped. "Every single dream line will be susceptible to Nightmares. Not dark dreams—Nightmares!"

"Even the Daydream Line," Alice finished. Her voice was gentle, but her words bit into Stella like teeth.

"Don't you see?" Anyway demanded as Stella continued to stare.

"If Nightmares intersect with Daydreams, they'll have a direct way into your world."

"But they can never make that line work," Spuddle reasoned.

"Why not?" Stella asked.

Anyway narrowed his eyes at What. "There isn't enough power to run it—"

The frog let out a very ugly, wheezing croak that was his version of a giggle.

Alice grabbed What by the throat. "Where are they getting the power, frog?" she demanded.

"Pirate," Anyway called. He had flipped over the map and now held it up for her to see.

Alice's eyes narrowed. "What is that?" she asked, plucking the paper from Anyway's paws and looking at it carefully.

Stella peered over her shoulder. "It's a transformer," she said. "It takes energy from these"—she pointed—"magnifies it and converts it to power, here. But—what are these things?" Stella studied the diagram.

"Ask . . . Stella's . . . brother—" What rasped.

"What?" Stella shrieked, lunging for him.

With a flailing kick, he wriggled out of Alice's grasp. Stella reached for him, but he had already hopped through the doorway and back into the clearing, where he dived into a bank of snowy paper.

"Stella—don't!" Anyway shouted, but Stella had already dived after him. The confetti was a deep cloud, and Stella swam through it, pulling herself deeper and deeper. Suddenly, a scrap of paper was before her eyes.

She had lost sight of the frog; she had lost sight of everything but the scrap—another with her brother's scrawl.

Deep in the dream,
The whiteness erases my words,
I grasp phrases
Like a buoy.
I struggle with a riptide
Of words meaning nothing.
The truth hides in the spaces
Between words, between letters . . .
I call your name,
But still I sink. . . .

PAJAMA DAY

The phone was ringing.

Stella opened her eyes to color, to shapes. She was back in her room. The whole Dreamway had disappeared in the light of day.

The ringtone jangled, and Stella picked it up. *Favorite Friend*, the caller ID read. Renee had stolen Stella's phone and programmed it herself.

"Hello?" Stella said groggily.

"Hello, hello—it's your favorite friend!" Renee chirped.

Stella took a deep breath and coughed. "Yeah—my caller ID told me."

"You weren't answering my texts!"

"I just woke up." Stella glanced at the clock. 7:05.

Late! She should have left for school five minutes ago.

"Well, this is a friendly reminder that today's theme is Pajama Day," Renee prompted.

Stella groaned.

"What? That should be easy! Just roll out of bed!"

"Yeah—that's lucky." Stella kicked off her flip-flops. "Okay, I'm coming. Thanks for the reminder!" She clicked off and grabbed a fresh set of pajamas. They were ancient and flannel and covered in purple cows. Deciding that bedhead was perfectly appropriate for this particular Spirit Day, she dashed into the kitchen and grabbed a granola bar.

Hearing the noise, her mother hurried into the kitchen. "I was beginning to wonder!" Tamara said. "You have money for lunch? You won't have time to pack it."

Stella nodded. She had the still-wrapped granola bar in her teeth and was frantically packing notebooks and papers into her backpack. She tossed the granola bar on top and said, "Any word?"

"Not yet," her mother replied.

Stella nodded grimly. Her father still hadn't called.

The unit was still in blackout. Half of her brain was sending her helpful messages like: *Don't read anything into it. He's been gone this long before.*

The other half of her brain was pure dread.

"You'll need to rush," Tamara said.

"Cole's left already?"

Tamara looked around, her gaze vague. "I suppose." She wrinkled her brow as if trying to remember something she couldn't quite call to mind.

The world tipped below Stella's feet—she had the oddest sensation that Reality was rearranging itself. That Cole was not only disappearing, he was being erased from the real world, so that when he was gone, nothing would be left—not even a memory.

I need to get back to the Dreamway, she thought. *I need to get back now.*

There was only one person who could help.

★

Even though she was only twenty minutes behind her usual time, the commute to school felt strange. The subway was more crowded, for one thing, and Stella was crammed into a seat between a woman with a backpack the size of a refrigerator and a man whose knees needed a minimum of a yard and a half between them at all times.

As she half dashed, half staggered up the street, she remembered how easy movement was on the Dreamway. It was frustrating to move so slowly when she needed to hurry.

Up on the street, she spotted a familiar figure. "Ms. Slaughter!" she called. When the librarian turned, Stella stopped in her tracks. Ms. Slaughter had been talking to . . . Angry Pete? Stella lurched forward uncertainly.

"Oh, hi, Stella," the librarian said smoothly. "On your way to school? I'd better get going too. I'll see you, Pedro."

"See you, Nancy," Angry Pete replied. He bent to pluck a dead bud from a marigold plant. He didn't scowl or say anything else.

Ms. Slaughter—Nancy, apparently—checked her watch as she and Stella walked the last two blocks to school. "Sorry," Stella said after a while. "I'm a little slow."

"I have first period free," she said to Stella. "There's no rush."

"How do you, uh—know that guy?"

"Pedro? He used to be an art teacher."

"He used to work with *kids*?" Stella asked.

"He used to work at Stringwood." Ms. Slaughter's mouth set into a grim line. "It was a few years ago. So—" Her voice took on the cheerful tone of a person who does not want to be asked more questions. "What makes you late this morning?"

"It took a long time to pick out the perfect pajamas," Stella replied, indicating her ratty purple cows.

"I forgot all about Pajama Day," Ms. Slaughter confessed.

"I have a reminder service," Stella told her.

★

Stella ducked into first-period math and handed the tardy slip to Mr. Ducklet, who was standing at the front of the class wearing a yellow bathrobe.

"Ah, the office staff is doing their job," he said with an amused twitch of his silver moustache. "I'll just add this to my collection." He tossed it in the trash. "Have a seat, Stella, and welcome to the wonderful world of calculating the area of a rhombus! It's—un*paralleled*." The class groaned, right on cue.

Renee gave Stella a horrified look that contrasted with her pajama top, which proudly declared, "Ready for some Zzzzs!" in sparkly letters. Stella couldn't quite decipher the look as she slipped into her usual seat. A few minutes later, Ramlah asked a question, and when Mr. Ducklet went to the board to answer it, Renee passed Stella a note.

Cole not in school. Sick?

Stella looked up from the note and saw that Renee wore a wide-eyed, frightened look. She felt the shadows gathering at the corner of the room behind her, but when Stella turned to look, she didn't see anything unusual. Just the despondent oatmeal walls, the slightly sagging bookshelf, and Mr. Ducklet's Wall of Fame, where he posted any test with a score of 95 or higher.

After the bell rang, Stella leaned over to Renee's desk. "Cole isn't here?"

Renee gave her a furtive look over the tops of her purple-framed glasses. She gathered her things and then motioned for Stella to head out into the hallway with her.

"What happened?" Stella asked as they fell into step. "Where's Cole?"

"I don't know!" Renee whispered. "It was so weird. He wasn't in homeroom, and when Ms. Jefferson was taking roll, she *skipped his name*. I pointed it out and she said, 'Oh?' and looked down at her list. And then someone asked a question, and—I think she forgot all about it!"

"So they haven't called my mom?" Stella felt time standing behind her, watching.

"I don't know! But, Stella—that's not the freaky part. I think he . . . he, like, went out."

"You saw him leave?"

"No—I think I saw him go out. Like a flashlight. Click. After homeroom, I saw him standing by the boys' room, and then, like—blink. Not there. I know that sounds crazy—he just went into the bathroom, right?" Her face was full of fear and confusion.

"Yeah, of course." Stella's mind whirled. She didn't know what to do. She had to find Alice, but she didn't know where she would be until the period after this one. *I have to wait,* she told herself, although the thought itself nearly made her jump out of her skin.

Stella was silent as she walked into class. She didn't look at anyone as she made her way to her desk. She looked straight through the classroom and out the window, where the gingko tree stood, still and empty.

When her French class was over, Stella did not bother going to gym.

"Just tell Coach Thuy that I'm at the library," Stella told Renee.

"Rope climbing is over, remember?"

"Tell her I broke my foot," Stella insisted. "Say anything. I've got to go to the library."

"I'll tell her you might have caught what your brother has and didn't want to do anything too strenuous—"

"Yes, fine," Stella told her. "Whatever." She gave her best friend, who was still formulating the perfect excuse, a quick hug and hurried down the hall.

When she arrived at the library, Alice wasn't there.

"Hello again," Ms. Slaughter said brightly. She was

shelving books near the back of the library.

Stella waved and gave a distracted smile. She waited until Ms. Slaughter disappeared between two tall rows of books, and then turned toward the librarian's desk. She looked at the mural, and for a moment she remembered seeing a small mouse on the day she had the seizure. But had that been real? Or had she imagined it?

Sensing someone behind her, she turned and found Alice looking up at the mural. "I knew you'd be here today," Alice said. Her pajamas were a white T-shirt top and pink pants with doughnuts on them. They somehow managed to be both cool and funny—and pajamas.

"It's all real, isn't it?" Stella asked.

Alice nodded once.

"Cole has disappeared. I have to go back. Right now," Stella said. "Can you teach me how?"

"I . . . don't know," Alice admitted. "But . . . I might be able to bring you along."

"What do you mean?"

"We're both . . . different. We've both been in that place between the waking world and the Dreamway. The liminal space. Me, when this happened"—she glanced down at her wheelchair—"and you, I assume when . . ." Her eyes cut to Stella's lame hand.

"Um . . ."

"The Space Between," Alice said quickly. "We're different. I told you before, I can stay as long as I want. And when I was holding your hand in the Dreamway, I managed to keep you there too."

Stella nodded. "I was almost pulled out when I read my brother's poem. You were the reason it didn't happen. And here—that day I had the seizure—"

"I think I did the same thing, only in reverse. You were heading off into the Dreamway, but—I kept you here."

Stella thought this over. "So maybe you could go now and bring me with you?" she asked.

Alice shrugged. "I've never tried it. But if there was a doorway . . ." They both looked up at the mural.

"It's different," Stella said. In the murky light, the mirror pieces whispered their shimmer, reflecting only the dim beams that stretched toward the glass from the faraway double doors. Usually, the scene reflected a bright, sunny day, but the light changed everything.

The sky behind the bridge looked gray, and the glass made the whole thing seem slick, as if it had just rained.

"It might work," Alice said, looking up at the scene. Her voice was darker, too, as if the light had changed it.

"Should we—should we hold hands, or something?" Stella asked.

Alice shrugged. "I guess." She reached out.

Her palm was wide, the fingers muscular. When you didn't know her well, Alice appeared delicate, almost frail. Her face was sharp-featured and her arms were slender. But she had a Pirate's hands, that was sure—hands for opening closed places, for taking what was not hers. It was a solid hand, and Stella felt safe holding it.

"One . . ." Alice said. She took a deep breath. "Two . . ."

"Three!" Stella cried. Running forward, she slammed into the wall, yanking Alice half out of her chair.

Alice lifted her eyebrows at Stella. "What was that?"

With a wince, Stella rolled onto her side and pushed herself up. "Uh—that's not what we're doing?"

"Are you okay?" Ms. Slaughter poked her head around the wall of shelves.

"I . . . tripped," Stella said, scrambling to her feet.

She and Alice both waved cheerfully. Ms. Slaughter shot them a suspicious glance before returning to her shelving cart.

Stella rubbed her arm. "Was—was something supposed to happen?"

"Well—I was hoping to see—" Alice stared at the mosaic. "Maybe we don't need to hold hands. Maybe we should . . ."

Stella waited for her to finish the sentence. "What?" she asked after a moment. "What?"

Alice shushed her. She was staring intently at the edge of the painting. "Wait," she whispered, continuing to stare.

Following her gaze, Stella noticed for the first time that the bridge in the mosaic continued, becoming a road and disappearing into the horizon. Behind her, beyond the library windows, a thick cloud passed over the sun, turning the scene a shade darker. Before, it had looked like a bridge on a cloudy day. The kind with a strong wind that would shake and rattle the leaves on the trees. Now, out of the corner of her eye, Stella could almost imagine that she saw actual rain and that the tree branches overhanging the bridge swayed.

"It's coming," Alice whispered, and Stella realized that there was now a car on the bridge. And the car was moving.

The silver sedan drove toward them, heading for the span. Stella was just about to ask something. She wasn't sure what, but she never spoke the words because Alice turned her head to look in the other direction.

A white truck was also on the road, heading toward the bridge.

"Step back," Alice said, and when Stella did, she realized that there was mud beneath her feet and all over her shoes, in fact.

"What—"

"It's raining," Alice said, and it was. Water streamed down Stella's face, and when she turned to look behind her, Stella saw that they were no longer in school. The mural, too, had changed. It was no longer a bridge in the countryside, but rather on a city street. The metal bridge, painted green, squatted like a praying mantis over dark water. The vehicles were still in motion.

Alice stood beside Stella, her eyes trained on the bridge, her wheelchair nowhere in sight. "Don't watch." Alice's voice was a command, but her eyes didn't leave the bridge.

Stella had to watch.

As the vehicles neared the bridge, the truck skidded around a curve.

"He's going too fast," Stella said as the sedan rolled up the side of the bridge. There was a woman behind the wheel and a child in the back seat.

The truck started over the bridge, too fast—much too fast—skidding again.

"Watch out!" Stella screamed, but the truck had already swiped along the edge of the sedan. The silver car burst through the guardrails, blasting through the concrete and plunging, headfirst, into the water below. "Help!" Stella screamed, running toward the river. "Oh my god!"

The man yanked open the door of the pickup truck and raced to the edge of the bridge.

"Help them!" Stella screamed at him. "Help them!"

He didn't seem to hear her, but he jumped.

"Let's go," Alice said.

"Let's go?!"

Alice gave her a long look. "You can't help them."

"What?" Stella screeched. "We have to!"

Alice looked her full in the face. "You can't help them," she said simply. "You can't help any of them."

Stella stared at the churning water where the car was slowly sinking. The man's head blasted out of the water, then disappeared again. "I have to know if they're okay!" she shouted after Alice, who stopped in her tracks. She turned slowly. Her eyes traveled to where the man desperately dove again.

"He saves the little girl. But her legs are crushed." Alice's voice was low. "The woman dies."

A chill settled over her. Rain pelted her face, and Alice's, and Stella wasn't sure if either of them was crying. "How do you know?" she whispered.

Alice stood still as stone. She closed her eyes.

"It's your dream," Stella said, and Alice's eyes snapped back open. They locked onto Stella's. A million years seemed to pass between them—time and space opened up, and then closed again, leaving a tight seam, like a scar, knitting them together.

"We made it," Alice said simply. "We're back on the Memory Line."

THE PATH

THE RAIN FELL STEADILY AS they tramped through the scrubby grasses of the open field. The scene did not look real to Stella. It looked, rather, like a charcoal drawing, softly smudged. She wondered if this was because it was built from Alice's memory. But it sounded real, and it felt real. Behind them, blue police lights flashed.

"Where are we going?" Stella asked after a while.

"We're out of that dream now," Alice replied. "We'll be at the tracks soon."

"Do you know where they are?"

"Yes."

"Have you . . ." Stella hesitated, ". . . have you been here before?"

"This is how I always get in."

The cold wetness on Stella's skin traveled down to her bones. "*This* dream?"

Alice did not stop walking; she didn't even slow her pace. "I'm sorry I had to bring you this way—"

"But you've never gone through the mosaic before—"

"Every door leads to the same place for me."

Nausea traveled up Stella's throat. Alice could come and go from the Dreamway whenever she wanted—but only by reliving the accident that had put her in a wheelchair. It rattled her very bones.

"Who was the woman?" Stella asked. "The one driving the car?"

This was the question that finally made Alice stop. She paused, just for a moment, although she didn't look at Stella. "My mother," she whispered. And then she moved on, forward through the darkness and rain, while Stella felt as if her heart had been ground to fine powder.

Stella and Alice had shared space in a school for almost a year. Stella had heard so many rumors about Alice, and she had never known which—if any—to believe. And now, here she was, seeing into Alice's secret dreams. Stella sank down onto the ground. Alice sat beside her, staring straight ahead. "Why do you come here?" Stella asked.

Alice was silent.

"You're the Pirate," Stella said slowly. "You search through discarded dreams, through Dross that should be recycled. You're . . . looking for something."

Alice's hands shifted so that her fingers were over her eyes.

"You don't have to tell me—"

"It's a necklace," Alice whispered. "The last time I saw it was during the accident. My mother gave it to me for my tenth birthday—it had been hers. I heard they removed it when I was in the hospital, and I never saw it again." She wiped her hands across her face and looked at Stella with weary eyes. "But it always showed up in my dream. Always. Until the first day I crossed paths with the Nightmare Line. That's when I lost it. But I thought that maybe it had been recycled, or maybe someone else had picked it up, or maybe it had been put in the Lost and Found. . . ."

Stella touched the silver necklace that hung around her neck. She wrapped her finger around the chain and pulled, so that it hung in front of her shirt.

Alice stared at the necklace. She reached out with tentative fingers as Stella unhooked it. "I thought I recognized the symbol on the pendant," Stella explained.

"Where—"

"We found it with the things marked Undisclosed." Stella helped Alice fasten it around her neck. Alice placed her hand over the pendant and closed her eyes.

"You made it out," Stella said at last. "Out of the Nightmare Line even though you came in as a non-sleeper."

"Yes."

"So—it can happen. It really can happen."

Neither girl spoke for a few moments. The only sound was of the steady rain. And then: a metal *clank*.

"They've found us!" Alice stood and began to run. Stella ran, too, and a moment later, they saw a flashing golden gleam. A terrified-looking mouse clung to the back of a clacking dragonfly as he fluttered drunkenly under the mouse's weight. Stella thought that she had never been happier to see anyone in her life.

"We're right by the tracks!" Anyway cried. "They're close!"

Alice nodded. She squinted, looking toward the woods that lurked just ahead of them. There was a clearing in the trees, and Stella could see that two silver rails traveled through the space between. For some reason, knowing that the line led across the dark woods filled Stella with a sense of dread.

Alice looked grim. "I guess we're here."

THE NIGHTMARE LINE

In the beginning, before the birth of the world, there was Darkness. Every darkness that exists today contains a tiny fleck of this ancient Darkness, the kind that exists beyond time. This Darkness is its own wisdom, and it has no thoughts or cares for humans. It is ruthless, this Nothing. It does not destroy. It simply negates. It denies. It existed before the beginning, and there will be Darkness after the ending, beyond the last world.

This is the Darkness that lies at the root of the Nightmare Line.

The moment Stella stepped into the woods, the air changed. It felt heavier, colder. It practically slithered across Stella's scalp with moist, frigid fingers. The trees reached overhead like giants with long, ropy arms. But the worst thing was the mist.

It was thin and seemed to gather at the base of the trees or the crooks of the branches. But it also seemed to creep inside Stella's body, slinking into her nose and filling her chest with a heavy darkness. It seeped into her arms and down her legs. It seeped into her *mind*, making her thoughts thick and stumbling. She was glad that Spuddle flew ahead, bright and spry, now that Anyway was back in her pocket. The nervous dragon-fly was a cheerful spot of color in the gloom.

Something moved in a nearby tree, and Stella's eyes darted toward the movement. She caught the barest glimpse of a black, prickly spider as it slipped into a hole in the tree's trunk. Stella let out a breath, and it appeared as a puff of gray air.

They walked along the silver rails, which were everywhere overhung with branches and vines. Rotted leaves were soft underfoot, and Stella's nose was filled with a putrid odor.

"I've always hated this line," Anyway whispered.

"Well, then I guess it's lucky that they're building a new one," Alice snapped.

Anyway scoffed, "I'm not counting on it to be an improvement. Quite the opposite, in fact!"

Overhead, the trees murmured and rustled.

"Do they talk to each other?" Stella asked. The branches seemed to pull together, like interlaced fingers tightening. But perhaps it was just a breeze or her imagination.

"Maybe," Alice replied.

Stella tried to stay close to Alice as she moved deeper into the shadows. At every step, the light grew dimmer, the mist colder. The rails went from silver to gray, from gray to black, twisting like scars across the forest floor.

It was a hopeless place.

But her brother was in here. He was here, somewhere. She had to find him. She scanned the ground, hoping to find another poem, perhaps another one of the missing pages from Cole's notebook.

Stella eyed the rails. She could almost feel the cold,

dark energy coming from them. In other parts of the Dreamway, the rails had seemed like proper steel—solid and stationary. These rails were silver, true, but had the sinewy glint of a sea creature that lived in a dark crevasse at the bottom of the ocean. She had the idea that they might just ooze in a whole different direction, if they felt like it. A third rail lay alongside them, looking cold and dead. "And—what will we do if a train comes along?" Stella asked. "We're not getting on it, are we?"

"No," Alice replied, moving ahead with the confidence of someone who had been here before and did not intend to stay long. "Riders on this line have nasty Dross. I was bitten by a wristwatch once." Scowling, she held a finger with a small, jagged white scar under Stella's nose. "Never. Again," she said emphatically, kicking a stone. Something small slithered away, showing only a glimpse of a black back with a red stripe before disappearing into the leaves. A moment later, the third rail sent up a shower of white-blue sparks that turned a worrying shade of venomous purple before dying away. The leaves did not rustle; the slithering thing was still. *I guess the third rail wasn't dead, after all*, Stella thought.

"We still don't know which stop we're headed for," Stella pointed out.

"Undisclosed," Alice said.

"What?"

"You saw the map—we have to find the *new* line. Which means we've got to get to the end of this line and cross over to the extension. Undisclosed. That's the stop where it happens."

"I just hope it isn't o-o-operational," Spuddle stutter-hiccupped.

"What difference does it make?" Alice asked.

"None," Anyway snapped.

"Of course it does," Stella shot back. "It makes a difference to *Cole*. He's disappeared from the Penumbra." Spuddle gasped, and suddenly Stella realized something horrible. "Are we . . . too late?" she whispered.

"No," Alice said.

"Maybe," Anyway admitted.

Spuddle hiccupped.

Stella turned to Anyway. "Is my brother gone for-ever? Am I going to forget him?"

Anyway shook his head.

"Am I?" Stella was nearly screaming.

"I don't know," Anyway admitted. "I just don't know."

Very, very deliberately, Stella placed Anyway on the ground. Then she started to walk away.

"Stella!" Alice called. "Stella—you can't just stalk off—it's the Nightmare Line!"

Stella wheeled on her. "I'm going to get my *brother*! I'm getting him right n—"

A faint *clang, clang, clank* rattled through the for-est. Then a small *toot* in an unsettling minor key.

"Excuse me," Spuddle said as Anyway and Alice craned their heads to look along the tracks.

"It wasn't you," Anyway told him as the rhythmic hiss drew nearer.

It was a train car, covered in dead, black vines and leaves that rattled like a witch's jewelry. The windows were dark, but one was open. It appeared to glower with a dangerous gleam, as if dreaming of gobbling them up. As it neared, Stella reached for Anyway and put him back into her pocket. The train car rolled up next to them and came to a stop that seemed utterly final.

"We're not getting on," Anyway announced. "Just in case anyone was wondering."

"It looks like it's been here a hundred years," Stella pointed out.

"I don't see a driver." Spuddle pulled out a small notebook and scribbled. "Another thing to report."

"I'm going in," Alice announced, striding toward the open window.

"What?" Stella cried.

"Do not mention that name," Anyway snarled. "Never speak of that frog again!"

"Stop!" Stella shouted, but it was too late—Alice had hauled herself up, and now she was nothing but a pair of legs disappearing inside the car. A moment later, her head appeared. "I'm just having a look," she said. "Back in a second."

Rushing over, Stella called, "Alice, this is not a good idea!"

"Would you please relax? This will only take a minute!" And her face disappeared from the open space.

Stella stood beside the train car, biting her thumbnail and frowning.

Here is the thing about people: just because you are saying something sensible does not mean that they will listen to you. Now, it seemed fairly obvious to Stella that any train car on the Nightmare Line should be left as alone as possible, if not more so. And perhaps this was obvious to Alice too. Nevertheless, that's not what she did, and this made so little sense to Stella that she found it infuriating. This reminded her of Cole and of how she had told him not to go down onto the tracks, and then she had told him not to go after that dog, which—it turned out—was not a dog at all but a Chimerath, and if he had only listened to her, he wouldn't have been kidnapped, and she wouldn't be here in this situation, standing by an evil witch's idea of a subway car in a Nightmare Forest.

Just as she was getting really worked up about it, the window slammed shut and the subway car began to move.

FALLING UP

ALICE'S SMALL FIST POUNDED AGAINST the scratched-up window from inside, but Stella didn't have time to think—just react. Racing after the car, she managed to catch the handle of the rear door. She hauled herself up to hook the edge of the doorway with her feet and clung there, spiderlike, as the train picked up speed.

"This is going well," said a voice from her pocket.

"Shut up," Stella growled at Anyway.

Stella could hear Alice banging away inside, like a bumper car in a junkyard. Alice wasn't the screaming type. "Alice!" Stella shouted.

Spuddle, who had been riding on top of the train car, zipped down and clung to the handle. "Um, excuse me—"

"Not a good time, Spuddle," Stella told him.

"Oh, sorry, okay." He zoomed back to the roof of the car.

"Alice!" Stella shouted again. "I'm here! I'll help you!"

The crashing stopped for a moment. Then Alice cried, "Well, what's the plan, then?"

"Working on it!" Stella said.

"It's almost as if she isn't grateful," Anyway said.

"Could you please be quiet unless you have something helpful to say?"

"Why don't you grab some of these vines?" Anyway suggested.

Stella grabbed one. It crumbled in her grip. "Next?" she grunted.

"I'm sorry to interrupt." Spuddle dipped and landed on Stella's shoulder.

"Still not a good time," Stella told him.

"All right." He zipped back up to the top of the train.

Her fingers strained at the edge of the door ledge; her toes ached in the tiny crevasse that held them. She could hear a furious Alice cursing inside the car. She had a very creative vocabulary. "Grab the emergency brake!" Stella shouted.

"There isn't an emergency brake!" Alice screamed back.

"Of course there is!" Stella cried. "There has to be!"

"This is a subway car in the middle of a Nightmare Forest on the Nightmare Line!" Alice countered. "It doesn't have a brake! I feel like that's kind of the point!"

Spuddle chose that moment to land once again on Stella's shoulder. "I'm afraid that what I have to tell you really can't wait," he announced.

Stella blinked at him. "Go ahead."

"Um, the tracks end in about a hundred yards," he said. "At the edge of a cliff."

Stella gaped at him.

"I thought you should know."

"Thank you, Spuddle," Anyway said from her pocket. "That was very helpful."

Spuddle smiled and curled his tail at the compliment. Then he darted away.

Stella's mind spun. There had to be an emergency

brake. All subway cars had an emergency brake, and so far, every one she had traveled in on the Dreamway had been like the ones in real life. They were made of scraps from her mind, after all, pieces of her imagination. And, while Stella didn't care much for stories, she understood mechanical things. All trains need an emergency brake, she told herself. Even a Nightmare train doesn't want to get into a smashup. Not on purpose, anyway.

Every fiber of Stella's body was concentrated on clinging to the exterior of the Nightmare train as it rattled and bucked over the tracks. A stray branch tottered off the roof, nicking her on the cheek. But Stella paid no attention. She ignored the grasping trees as they reached out for her. Her mind was in a different place entirely: she was inside the subway car; she was remembering what an emergency brake looks like. There had to be one. There had to be.

"Fifty yards!" Spuddle shouted.

It's red, Stella thought, bright, like a fire engine. And rectangular, made of metal, and with a handle wide enough to fit all your fingers through. STOP was painted in white block letters about an inch high. She held this in her mind, held it there with as much strength as she held on to the car with her fingers.

Alice let out a shout, and a moment later, the universe began to scream. The brakes engaged and the subway car convulsed, bucking like a cat that someone has forced into a costume. Light flickered on the dead branches on either side as the brakes screeched, sending up sparks in a silver shower that looked like a fiery lawn sprinkler.

"We're not stopping!" Spuddle shouted. "Twenty yards!"

Still, Stella clung to the end of the car. In her mind, she knew that tracks did not simply end. There would be a safety stop—a pylon, something concrete, something that would keep a train from going over the edge. . . .

"Ten yards!"

"We're slowing down!" Anyway cried.

"Not enough!" Spuddle screeched.

Anyway burrowed down into her pocket, but Stella did not cover or even close her eyes. She looked around, frantically searching the edge of the forest for a solution, some way to slow the train. That is why her eyes were open to see a figure move in a tree twenty yards ahead. A moment later, a large black branch crashed onto the tracks. The train car slammed into it, and the wood jammed between the wheels and the rails.

The train car screech trailed to a scraping wail and suddenly bucked, sending Stella flying. She landed on her shoulder between the tracks. Gravel scraped her skin as she scrambled to her knees.

The subway car squatted, motionless, before her.

"What happened?" Spuddle asked. He looked out over the vast cliff before them. "Is this heaven?"

"Owwww," groaned a voice from the other side of the subway door.

"Alice! Are you okay?" Stella shouted.

In response, the rear emergency exit door slid open. Alice stood in the doorway looking like someone who had just arm-wrestled a tornado. Her eyes closed slowly, then snapped open. "I'm trying to think of a witty reply to that question," Alice admitted, "but I think my brain got scrambled."

"Oh, you're so lucky!" Spuddle announced, flitting over to Alice. "Thank goodness for that branch!"

But it wasn't luck. Stella knew it wasn't. She turned her gaze toward the tree and saw the dark shape crawling down the trunk.

Anyway noticed her expression. "What is it?" he asked as the large, dark shape landed at the base of the tree and started to move away.

"Who's there?" Stella shouted, and the figure froze. "Who is that?"

The figure stepped out of the shadows, and Stella saw him clearly for the first time. It was a man wearing jeans and a filthy hooded sweatshirt. His dark eyes flashed with intelligence, not anger, as they gazed out from beneath long gray curls. "It's nobody," the man said. "Nobody to be afraid of, anyway," he added.

"Angry Pete?" Stella asked slowly.

He didn't reply.

She tried again. "Pedro?"

He studied her face, his expression a question mark.

"You know my librarian," Stella explained. "Nancy Slaughter."

"Oh." Pedro looked confused.

"You—saved us. Thank you."

Pedro shrugged. "Nobody deserves to be on that train," he said simply.

"How long have you—been here?" Stella asked.

Pedro looked around. "Long time," he said finally. "A very long time, I think."

"How did you get here?" Anyway asked. "You're not even properly in a dream, and you're not on a train—"

"I found a way out of my dream," Pedro said slowly. "But I can't seem to find my way out of here. Been in the forest, seems like . . . forever. No way out."

"It's that way." Alice pointed toward the Memory Line, the direction they had come from.

Pedro's eyes held hers for a moment. Then he glanced over her shoulder and shuddered. "No."

"She's right," Anyway assured him. "The only way for you to get out is through the Memory Line. . . ."

"I'm not going that way," Pedro said simply.

"You have to," Stella said softly. "You don't want to stay here, do you?"

Angry Pete glared at her. "Of course I don't want to stay here."

"All right, so then—" she prompted.

"There's things worse than this," Angry Pete replied. His voice was a low growl, a warning. "Plenty worse."

The forest around them was silent, as if it were watching them. Stella wondered what horrors lurked in its depths and how it could possibly be less frightening than what Pedro might find on the Memory Line. Whatever that was, she realized, it must be *horrible*.

Her heart ached for Pedro, and she realized that she could never be afraid of him again—not when he was so full of fear himself.

"Do you know about the new Nightmare Line?" Stella asked, making her voice as gentle as she could. "Have you seen it?"

His dark eyes grew guarded. "I've seen something," he told them. "Don't know what it is. But I'm not going in that direction, either. I'd rather stick to the woods."

"How do we get there?" Stella asked.

"Don't know how you get there," Angry Pete replied. He turned away from her slowly and pointed toward the horizon. "But if you're looking for it, there it is."

ALL SOULS

"LOOKS LIKE TERRIBLE WEATHER," SPUDDLE observed. "And me without an umbrella."

Far above them, but still low in the sky, a cauldron of gunmetal clouds skulked and writhed. They seemed to hum, heavy and charged. As the four friends watched, a small spark of lightning flared in the depths.

There was something strange about those clouds, Stella realized. But she couldn't figure out what it was. She turned to ask Pedro about it, but he was already disappearing into the depths of the forest.

"Pedro!" she called. "Pedro!" He did not slow down or even look back, and it made her shiver. It had not occurred to her before that moment that—perhaps—Cole wouldn't *want* to leave the Dreamway. She turned toward the clouds, feeling a shadow of dread fall across her heart.

"That's not weather." Anyway's voice was low and careful.

Stella's mind, which had been busily trying to understand the clouds, finally managed to form them into a shape that made sense. After a moment, she gasped.

The clouds were not, in fact, clouds at all. It was a black vortex, like a puncture wound in the sky.

At the edge of the blackness hulked a collection of machinery clumped together to form a ring roughly the size of a baseball field and approximately the same shape as a large intestine. It looked cold and slimy, like the skin of an octopus, and—although it was, in fact, a machine that made up that circle—Stella had the uncomfortable feeling that it was *alive*. She felt as if it were looking at her and didn't think much of what it saw . . . except, perhaps, as a snack.

Anyway pulled out What's map and unfolded it. Then he turned it over to the diagram on the back and squinted.

Stella thought that the picture didn't look much like what was in front of them. But her father always said that a diagram is sometimes just a representation of what is supposed to *happen*. It isn't necessarily an illustration of what something *looks* like. She looked at the vortex and the machinery again. "It's the transformer," she said.

"That's what I was afraid of," Alice admitted.

"It looks like there's a way to get up to it," Anyway pointed out, "from the other side of the canyon."

"Okay!" Spuddle said brightly. "So let's go across!"

"That's easy for you," Stella snapped at the dragonfly. "You can fly. The rest of us have a problem."

"Well." Spuddle sounded hurt. "There is a bridge."

The others turned to have a look. To call this bridge "rickety" was to insult rickety bridges the world over. It looked like an art project by a three-year-old at nature camp—pointless string and sticks held together by ignorant tangles.

"Are we supposed to walk across that?" Stella asked. "It's impossible!" She turned to Anyway and Alice. "Tell him, you guys!"

Alice gave her a level look. "Just because it's impossible doesn't mean that it can't be done."

"Yes it does," Stella cried. "That is literally what it means!"

"Stop being literal," Alice told her. She pointed at her own stony expression. "Does this face look literal to you? Does this *place* look literal to you?"

"I have no idea how to answer that," Stella replied. She looked back at the bridge. Part of her thought that there had to be another way.

But even if there is, she realized, *we're running out of time. We might already be too late!* She had to get to Cole, even if it was dangerous. With a deep breath, she took a step forward.

"I'll go first," Anyway announced.

"You *are* the lightest," Spuddle agreed.

Anyway glared at him. "I think you mean, 'No, no, Anyway, don't be foolish! I would be devastated if something terrible happened to you.'"

"It'll be fine! You just have to trust!" Spuddle insisted. "It's the one thing they never expect in places like this!"

Anyway scrambled down from Stella's pocket and hopped over to the bridge. He stood at the edge for a long time. Finally, he put one tentative paw out and tested the rope. "Seems . . . okay," he said dubiously. He climbed out. "It's . . . pretty sturdy, actually." He went a bit farther. "Much stronger than it looks." He bounced up and down a few times.

"I'll try," Alice said, and strode over to the bridge. There were two ropes, one at the height of each of her shoulders. She held on to these and placed a foot carefully on the twig and rope deck. She stepped out, balancing cautiously, gripping the hand ropes with white knuckles. After a few steps, she seemed to relax a bit. "Stella, Anyway is right—it's better than it looks. Come on!"

Stella was afraid of heights, and the rickety bridge looked alarmingly like something her brain had cooked up deliberately to scare her to death. "It's a dream," she told herself as she walked to the edge. "It's only trying to frighten you." She stepped out. The rope bridge swayed and sank a few inches under her weight, but did not creak, groan, or make any other alarming noises.

It isn't very hard to balance on a tightrope when you have something to cling to, but it can get challenging when the rope is not tight and neither are the things you're grasping. There were a lot of "whoas" and "yikeses," but with some awkward flailing and pulling and splayed legs and arms, Stella centimetered (inched was too strong a word) her way across the crevasse. The diagram sat tucked safely in her pocket as she shuffled awkwardly forward. The bridge was narrow; each foot had to be placed directly in front of the foot behind. Stella tripped once, sending the bridge swaying.

Alice and Anyway let out a shout and clung to the sides.

"Sorry!" Stella called.

"No problem," Alice said over her shoulder. "Just move slowly."

"That's how I always move," Stella replied. She was grateful that her arms and legs had more freedom in the Dreamway. In the real world, she never could have managed the crossing.

It was relatively easy passage for Anyway, who could simply scamper in his usual way. He could cling to the ropes with all four feet.

"Oh, this is wonderful!" Spuddle said as he buzzed near Stella's ear. "It's working out perfectly!"

"Stop being so chipper," Anyway grumbled.

"I'm encouraging you!" Spuddle insisted as he buzzed forward to join Anyway. "You're almost half-way along!"

"I don't want to be encouraged!" Anyway insisted. "Go encourage Alice."

But this only served to convince the dragonfly that he simply wasn't offering enough encouragement. "You can do it you can do it you can do it!" he chanted, all the while turning somersaults in the air near Anyway's head.

"Look—get off!" Anyway said, swatting at the fly.

"You're more than halfway there!" Spuddle did another flip.

Anyway stood on his hind legs and flapped his arms as Spuddle zipped past.

"Be careful, you two," Alice said, just as Stella tripped again.

The bridge swayed and there was a tiny "Ah!" as Anyway fell off and plunged into the darkness below.

"Anyway!" Steila shouted.

"Spuddle!" Alice cried. The dragonfly blasted downward after his friend, but Anyway was already rising. He floated past them, his arms and legs spread wide.

"Stop!" Stella shouted. "Stop!"

"I can't stop!" Anyway shouted. "I'm falling!"

"You're doing it wrong!" Spuddle shrieked as he raced after him. "Stop falling *up*!" Grabbing onto his tail, he tried to pull Anyway back downward. But the force of reverse gravity was too strong. Soon, they were both falling upward.

Alice turned to face Stella. "What do we do?" she asked.

The mouse and the dragonfly were rising—rising straight toward the mass of metal at the edge of the black hole. Toward an enormous, gaping opening. It yawned with huge, jagged edges, reminding Stella uncomfortably of a shark in a movie she had watched from behind the couch without her mother's knowledge. Stella's blood throbbed through her body, filling her head.

"They're going to go right in," she said aloud. "That's where we want to be."

"Are you saying—"

Stella didn't answer. Instead, she jumped.

"I was afraid of that," Alice muttered to herself.

A DOOR

THE AIR SLOWED AS ANYWAY, Spuddle, Alice, and Stella rose through an opening at the edge of the twisted circular machine. The inside was dark, but not black. It was the red of dark wine, and it seemed to throb as if the walls had a pulse. The air below them continued to blow, but it seemed to have reached its summit. They balanced there for a moment, like a ball balanced at the highest point on a fountain.

Stella leaped toward the ledge. "Let's go."

The ledge underfoot had an unpleasant texture. It was a bit squashy, like a thick exercise mat or, perhaps, a tongue. Overhead, taking up almost the entire hangar-size space, was the inky, churning vortex they'd seen from below. It sparkled with tiny lights. But these lights were not cheering—they were cold, each a single pinprick of fear connected to a nebula of wires. The center of the nebula emitted a terrifying sound, a screeching crunch and grind like the sound of bones caught in a wood chipper.

The spiral crouched overhead, flickering. It continued to grind and gurgle as the lights screamed with pained ferocity. Brilliant, almost blinding, flashes reflected against the red walls, making Stella's eyes hurt, making her ears ache, stabbing a hole in her heart. She had the feeling that the thing—whatever it was— wasn't quite alive, but wasn't quite dead, either, and it was being tortured. She was filled with revulsion and horror and wondered what might happen if she were sick. She swallowed the vomit rising in her throat and turned away, just in case.

"What is it?" Spuddle screeched, staring up at the hideous cyclone.

"I'm not sure." Alice's voice was slow and hesitant. "But I think they must be—"

"Souls," Anyway said.

★

What happens when a soul is tortured until it is snuffed out?

The thoughts loop, endlessly grinding, like gears that can't catch. They repeat, sending their excruciating messages in endless repetition until they drown out all other thoughts and erase emotions. Day by day, the person grows more and more withdrawn. Their eyes become haunted and their expression flattens until the roaring furnace hisses, dims, flickers, and finally—goes out.

This is not death. Death is what happens to the body in the waking world. When the spirit is crushed, it is a death that defies the power of life. You breathe, you eat, you sleep. And all of the time the Nightmares dwell inside of you, and any happy feeling or thought that tries to enter withers under the force of this power.

As Stella stood, looking at the vortex, she thought about how Cole had always had a light inside of him, but lately the light had been muted. She could almost see the thick veil of fog that circled his head like a corona. She thought about Angry Pete and how his eyes were blue but seemed like two dark holes leading to the bottom of an ancient well where nothing stirred. She thought of the way that he seemed to spout shadow, of the way she feared him before he had ever spoken to her. Stella knew that if she did not find Cole, the essence of him would fade—like a vibrant chalk drawing blurred and eventually washed away by rain.

"If it's a transformer—and I think it is—we can shut it down," Stella announced. She studied the spiral and the connecting wires, and suddenly remembered programming a basic circuit board with her father.

"This is the capacitor," he had explained, his long finger pointing. "It stores energy and then releases it."

Capacitor. Circuit. Transformer. Induction. Energy. Voltage. Her mind lit up, and she saw it at once.

"The transformer takes energy and magnifies it." Stella pulled What's diagram from her pocket and pointed to it. "For the new Nightmare Line—that's how they'll get the energy they need to power it."

"We'll smash it," Alice announced, but Stella caught her arm.

"Wait—wait," Stella's mind spun frantically. "So—the cloud is transforming soul energy. But where are the capacitors? The things that create the power?" Stella asked.

Alice, Spuddle, and Anyway stared blankly back at her. "Where are the people at the other end of the connecting wires?" she clarified. "Where is my *brother*? I see his energy up there, but where is *he*?"

They stood at the edge of a crater. The eddy swirled at the center, reaching down to unknown depths. A waterfall spilled from the edge of the crater, the water disappearing into the cyclone without a sound. Around the edge of the crater were seven caves. To the left of the waterfall, one of the caves formed a triangular A-frame. To the right, the cave was a straight column.

"If I had to bet, I'd say he's in one of those," Anyway told her.

"It'll take us forever to search them all!" Spuddle cried.

"We have to shut this down now," Alice repeated. "Look, I don't want to run into a Chimerath, or something worse, before we stop this thing."

They stared at the horrible writhing spiral arms. Stella's flesh squirmed at the sight. "What happens to

Cole if we shut it down?" she demanded. "Even if he gets out of the new Nightmare Line, he could end up lost and stuck on the old one. And he might never find his way out."

"What happens if we *don't* shut it down?" Alice shot back.

Stella's gaze returned to the openings. At that moment, Stella heard her name. The hideous noise was still billowing from the churning cloud, but she heard the voice clearly.

"Cole," she whispered. She looked at the caves, watching the waterfall, soundlessly, soundlessly. It fell forever.

"Just let me try to get him," she said. "I think I know where he is."

"What?" Spuddle cried. "How?"

"Look—my brother's poems, remember? He left them for me, like pebbles. A cave. Water. Sand and boulders. *The truth hides between letters. . . .*" She gestured toward the cave shaped like an A and the one shaped like an I—between them was the waterfall. "There has to be another cave behind that waterfall."

Alice looked shaken. "We have to stop *this*," she said, arms waving toward the giant transformer.

"Let me find him first," Stella begged.

Alice held her gaze for a long moment. Finally, she nodded. "Go as quickly as you can," she said.

"Don't do anything until I come back," Stella begged.

"I can't promise," Alice told her. "Just get him—fast."

★

The waterfall fell in a silver sheet, like rolled tin. But as they raced toward it, they could see that the cliff continued behind it.

"I—thought there would be a cave here," Stella said. "I was so sure of it."

"Then he's here," Anyway said.

"He isn't, though," Stella replied. "There's no entrance."

Anyway glanced up at her sharply, then looked back at the wall. "Why do you insist on being able to *see* everything?" he demanded.

Normally, Stella would have argued. But she didn't

have time for that and, more importantly, neither did Cole. He needed her. So she decided that—since logic didn't seem to matter much in the Dreamway—she would just skip the part where she insisted that reality could never work that way and get on with it. "How do I get inside?"

"You walk through," Anyway replied.

Stella took a cautious step. Then another and she was halfway through the rough rock wall. One more, and she was on the other side, standing at the end of a long hallway lined with many rooms. She raced down the hallway. Each room held a person. One woman stared blankly at the exit. One man was asleep on the floor. One girl was scribbling on the walls. None of them seemed aware of Stella. Stranger, none of them seemed to realize that they weren't being held there. There were no bars. No doors. It looked to Stella as though they could simply walk into the hallway and out toward the waterfall and be free.

Twelve rooms down, on the right, Stella saw a boy with black hair, slumped in a chair. He was thin and pale and weak looking, and it made Stella's heart sick to look at him. "Cole?" she whispered.

Cole didn't move.

"We're too late," Anyway whispered, and Stella darted forward only to run into a wall. She put out her hands, feeling along the invisible barrier, which was cold as ice. So cold it burned her skin. She looked down at Anyway. "Why do you insist on being able to see everything?" the mouse repeated, but this time, his voice held a note of sadness.

"Cole!" Stella shouted, and her brother's eyes fluttered open. They gazed out into the distance. "Stella?" he called hoarsely. "Where are you?"

"Cole!" she shrieked from the behind the clear blockade. "I'm here! I'm right here!"

"Where?" Cole wailed. "Stella, I can't see you! I can't move!"

Panic pooled into Stella's stomach, pumping through her veins, reaching every part of her body. "What's wrong with him?" Stella looked down at Anyway. "Why can't he see me?"

Anyway stared at the boy. "Ask him what he does see."

"Cole!" Stella cried. "Cole—where are you? What do you see?"

"I'm in the desert!" Cole shouted. He lifted his head and called toward the ceiling, as if he were at the bottom of a hole. "I'm standing on a land mine—if I step off, I'll explode!"

"Cole—Cole, listen to me—that isn't real," Stella shouted. "It isn't real. I can see you. You're here with me! In the middle of an empty—"

"It *is* real!" Cole shrieked. "Dad's here, but it's not him, Stella! He's coming for me! He's going to—" He let out a strangled cry, and Stella beat against the invisible walls, smashing it with her fists, slamming it with her whole body. "It's just fear, Cole! You're just afraid! You're trapped in a Nightmare!"

"Stella!" he screamed. "Help me!"

"It isn't real, Cole! Listen to me! It isn't real!"

Cole let out a hideous scream as Anyway ran frantically along the wall, trying desperately to find another opening, but there was none, visible or invisible.

"It isn't real! This kind of pain can't kill you!" Stella screamed.

"It is killing me. . . ." Cole sobbed. "It's killing me. . . ."

"Kill it back!" Stella cried. "You've got to kill it back!"

"I can't!" Cole groaned.

He was right there—right there, and Stella couldn't do anything to save him. He was going to have to save himself—but how? How could she get him to do it?

"You're brave," Stella said slowly. "Cole—you've always been the brave one."

"I'm tired," Cole whispered, weeping. "I don't want to be brave anymore."

"Just a little more," Stella replied. "I know you can. You're the one who told Mom and Dad when I was having a seizure. You're the one who told me stories all night when Dad was deployed. You stood up for me when Connor teased me. Please. Be brave a little more. Be brave for me. This is fear—just . . . feel it. Just *feel* it and then come grab my hand."

"How do I know that you're real?"

"You'll just have to trust," Stella replied. "You have to trust *me*."

Cole slumped to the floor, and Stella screamed. The chair fell with a metallic clang, and Cole wriggled to his knees. He choked and cried, placing a hand to his throat as he crawled forward. Stella was now pressed against the invisible wall with her whole body, heedless of the burning pain as her brother struggled forward. "I'm here!" she cried. "I'm right here!"

His knees slid forward. He gasped and cried, one hand reaching for her, the other hand to his throat.

"I won't leave!" Stella whispered. "I'm here!"

Agony tore at her, her skin burned, she felt as if her chest were breaking open as she watched her brother struggle. He drew closer, she could see his black eyes. They blinked and stared, not seeing her—caught in their own visions as Cole recoiled from some invisible horror.

He was close now—not more than a foot away.

"I'm here," Stella said. "Reach out."

His eyes were wide with horror. "I can't—"

He didn't move. He was perfectly still—almost hypnotized.

"Hold me in your mind, Cole," Stella said. "You

don't have to see me to know I'm real. Just remember me. Think of Mom . . . and Dad . . . and Aunt Gertie and Renee . . . Remember us."

Tentatively, like a sprout struggling through the dark earth to reach the light, Cole reached out. His fingertip touched the other side of the wall.

Stella leaned forward and placed her finger on her side. Then she pressed her whole palm against the wall, whispering, "I'm here. I'm right here. You can see me in your mind."

He pressed his finger against the barrier, and suddenly, instead of the frigid burn of the wall, she felt Cole's hand. It was cold and sweaty as she grabbed it and pulled him through, but it was his hand, his living hand. It was the real Cole. It was her brother.

His hand grew warmer, then hot, then searing, and as Stella pulled him into a hug, her body burned cold and the gray room disappeared, and she stepped right into Cole's dream.

★

The walls dissolved, and Stella was back in the desert. She screamed as the sky ripped open, crushing her beneath a wall of sound. Before her, flames licked toward the sky as Cole ran toward a dusty brown Jeep. It burned, bright and hot, but it was not consumed. The noise had deafened Stella, but she could read the word on her brother's lips: *Dad.*

We're in our father's desert, *she realized, and her mind raced.* What if it's real? What if Cole and I never wake up? What if reality has crossed over and we can't escape—ever?

Struggling, she staggered toward Cole and wrapped her arms around him. She held on to him as if she would never let go.

TRANSFORMER

STELLA'S FINGERS WERE STILL TOUCHING Cole's as the dream fell away. They were back in the Dreamway, and Cole was lying on the cold damp floor, looking up into Stella's face. He looked frightened and small, but it was him—the real him. "Stella?"

"It's me."

Cole looked around. "Where are we?"

"We're stuck in a Nightmare," Stella explained. "But I'm getting you out."

"I'm dreaming?" Cole asked.

"Not anymore," Anyway put in.

"Not exactly," Stella said.

"Did that mouse just talk?" Cole asked.

"Yes," Anyway and Stella said at the same time.

Cole blinked and looked around at the bare room. "This is where I was?" he asked. "There's nothing here."

Stella squeezed his fingers. "You were dreaming."

"It felt real."

"It *was* real," Stella said. "It *is* real." The floor gave a violent jerk beneath them, yanking Stella's heart against her chest. Anyway stared up at the ceiling. "Look out!" he cried as a chunk of metal rained down nearby. The floor shook again, this time more violently.

"What's that?" Cole asked, looking at Stella.

"We've got to go," she translated.

Cole looked at her carefully. Then he nodded. He struggled to stand on wobbly legs, and Stella hauled him to his feet and they staggered forward.

"Your leg," Cole said, staring.

"Things are different here," Stella told him.

"This way!" Anyway cried.

"Where are we going?"

"We can't get back out the way we came," Anyway pointed out. "Alice is shutting down the transformer.

We'll have to find our way out through the hallways!"

"Who's Alice?" Cole asked, but there was no time to answer.

As they raced past, Stella thought about the people trapped in the rooms upon rooms. "Anyway!" she called.

"We can't," he shouted. He didn't even need to hear what she had to say.

"What is it?" Cole asked.

Stella peered inside, where a girl sat on a chair, weeping as she gazed at something invisible on the floor. Stella wanted to help her, but she didn't know how.

"We have to." Stella's voice wasn't even pleading. It was a statement.

"We *can't*. They have to free themselves," Anyway called.

"But they'll still be lost on the Nightmare Line!" Stella insisted. "Like Angry Pete!"

"When the transformer shuts down, they should be able to walk out! They'll have a chance," Anyway replied. "That's more than they have now!"

The floor shook again, and a chunk of steel clanged down nearby. "I think Alice has figured it out," Stella called.

"Keep going!" Anyway replied.

They raced liked mad, plunging as fast as they could toward the beating heart of the new Nightmare Line, the transformer.

She could hear it—the ungodly screams from the transformer echoed down the hallway as the floor heaved and buckled again. The screams were lifted for a moment, and then silence. A hole in the noise. Why had it gone silent?

Cole and Stella staggered on—the quakes were coming more steadily now. A wall behind them collapsed in a screech of metal and concrete. The lights flickered, and they pulsed on again.

"Don't look back," the mouse commanded, and in the next moment, they were there—the transformer lay before them and below, sparks spewing from the center, the deafening howls reverberating through the space. Stella could see Alice on a promontory above, bashing at a panel in the wall with a piece of pipe. Meanwhile, sleek creatures the color of a dream at midnight sla-vered up the wall toward her.

Chimerath. They looked more solid than before, and Stella could see that they were stuck together, spare parts of people's horrors—black and terrible fangs, wings of leather, lean wolf body, and all of them changing, twisting as the minds they fed on served up worse and worse terrors. Spuddle flew toward one, but it batted him away. Stella could see what Alice was aim-ing for: a large black box lit with wires. A Chimerath reached Alice, who threw up her arm to protect her face as vicious eagle talons clamped down on her.

Cole stood, gaping at the churning hole, hypno-tized.

"We need to find a door!" Anyway shouted.

"Not yet!" Stella picked up a heavy chunk of con-crete the size of a grapefruit and raced to the nearest wall. She mounted a ladder set into the side and hauled herself upward until she reached the remains of a bridge. She hefted the chunk, took aim, and threw, but her footing slipped awkwardly as the transformer rocked with another convulsion. The rock flew wide of the mark, but one of the Chimerath spotted her. Snarling and growling, it galloped across the wall—half Nightmare horse, half spider—as Stella picked up another hunk of concrete and threw it.

The concrete chunk hit the black box squarely in the center, and sparks poured forth in a silver fountain. Alice wailed as the Chimerath crashed into Stella, knocking her backward. Her footing slipped, and she toppled, screaming "Run!" as she fell toward the swirling vortex.

★

She fell through the blackness for what seemed like days, or weeks, or years. She fell until time had no meaning, and only the darkness existed. She fell until she was not falling anymore—the darkness clung to her, and it was all around her, as if she was floating in deepest space. And then she saw it: a crack, a weak tendril of light.

She moved toward it, and it grew until it was wide enough for her to squeeze through. Stella held her breath and shimmied, and wriggled, and squirmed until she had left the darkness behind.

She stepped out into Nowhere.

There was the Metro stop, and there was the bench. And there, perched on the armrest, was Monseiur Bleu, her blue jay.

Bleu cocked his head at Stella.

"Where have you been?" she asked. And as she watched he grew and changed. His wings became strong arms, and his warm dark eyes flashed above a mischievous grin.

"Dad?" Stella asked.

He smiled.

"Are you safe?" she asked.

Her father sighed deeply. "No one is ever safe in this world," he said slowly. "Alice will tell you."

Stella did not know how to reply. She sat down beside him and they watched the sun creep toward the horizon, sending sparkles across the fountain. The lights on the Metro sign flickered on, glowing in the middle of Nowhere.

Stella turned toward her father, to see his face in the

golden light, but he had disappeared.

Ding.

Nearby, the elevator doors rattled open.

It had come for her.

THE LONG HALL

THE FIRST THING STELLA NOTICED was the unmistakable smell of books. She opened her eyes to see Alice staring down at her.

Stella was in the Stringwood library, lying on the particularly filthy carpet. She tried to push herself up on her right arm, fell backward, and then rolled over to her left side. "Are we back?" she asked. And then, without waiting for an answer, "Where's Cole?"

The library door flew open and Renee shouted, "Stella!"

"This is a library!" Ms. Slaughter warned, but Renee raced between the shelves, calling her friend's name.

"Here!" Stella shouted as Renee rounded the corner, glasses askew.

Renee stopped and stared. "Why are you on the floor?"

"I dropped my pencil," Alice said smoothly. "Stella was helping me get it."

"What's wrong?" Stella asked.

"Your mom is here."

Stella scrambled to her feet as her mother walked in through the door. "Mom—" She raced to Tamara, who wrapped her in a hug. "Mom, I can't find Cole—"

"It's all right—"

"No! It's not—he's not in class, and I think—"

"Stella." Her mother's gentle voice made her wince, and for a moment, she was afraid that Tamara would ask, "Who is Cole?" She feared that it was too late, that her brother, even his memory, was gone forever—

"Stella?" Cole said weakly. He stepped out from behind Tamara and put a hand on their mother's shoulder. Then he put another on Stella's, and she saw how tired he looked, how pale his face.

"He was in the nurse's office," Renee announced.

"Nurse Kendricks called me," Tamara explained. "I wanted to tell you that I'm taking Cole home."

Stella gaped at her brother, speechless.

"How do you feel?" Alice asked.

Cole looked at her, and in his eyes was a spark that burst into a small flame. *I remember you*, his glance said. "I feel . . . better." He formed his words carefully. "Thank you," he added, and his gaze fell back onto his sister.

Stella studied her brother's face. Although he was pale, his expression looked better than he had in days. He was the right mixture of light and shadow, and his eyes were clear.

Did he remember? Did he remember anything about the Dreamway? She would ask him one day. Not right now, not in front of Renee and their mom.

"You'll be okay," Alice said, and the silver necklace gleamed at her throat.

"How do you know?" Cole asked her.

"I guess I just have a feeling that you're like Stella. Stronger than you look."

Stella hooked her index right finger around Alice's. Then she hooked her left around Renee's. Renee reached for Cole. As they sat there linked, each by a single finger, Stella thought about the Dreamway, the horrors of the Nightmare Line, the wonder of falling up, the Green Man, and Alice's secret life as the Pirate. And she remembered, in her bones, how it felt to have the desperate Chimerath cling to her. But, together, they were strong enough to help her brother pull himself out of his nightmare.

Stella looked at her tired mother, who worked so hard and missed Stella's father and still managed to take care of them.

It would still be the same world, with the same fears and lurking shadows.

No one can ever be perfectly safe, Stella thought, but somehow she felt that was okay. Right now, right at this moment, things were okay.

She would wait for her father's call, and she had faith that it would come. And no matter what, they had each other.

"We're all a lot stronger than we look," Stella said as outside, beyond the library window, a blue jay fluttered, settling into his nest in the gingko tree.

ACKNOWLEDGMENTS

I would like to thank Kristen Pettit for her unflagging belief in this book. Her faith was the lighthouse that helped me navigate draft after draft. And I would like to thank Rosemary Stimola for her many blunt questions and dubious looks during the initial stages of this novel. When Rosemary finally said, "Well done," I knew that she meant it. Many thanks to Melissa Telzer, and to Ali, Zara, and Marmie.

AUTHOR'S NOTE

I know what it's like to be stuck in the Dreamway.

When I was in the fourth grade, I became what used to be called a latchkey kid. A latchkey is the key you use to get into a house from the outside. I had a key to my house that I kept on a string around my neck, hidden under my shirt. On days I had to use the key, my parents left shortly before I did. I would lock up the house and walk the quarter mile to school on my own. After school, I would walk home and let myself in. I was supposed to call one of my parents and then do my homework. Usually, what I would do was call one of my parents, and then drink a lot of root beer while watching my favorite television shows.

I never told anyone that being a latchkey kid terrified me.

I wasn't afraid that a stranger would try to get into the house or kidnap me. In fact, I wasn't afraid in the afternoons at all. I was afraid in the *mornings*. I was afraid that I would do something wrong—forget to lock the house or leave on the toaster—something that would cause us to get robbed or make the house burn down. I remember getting halfway to school and then running back home to make sure the house was locked. Sometimes, I would unlock the door and then relock it. Two blocks later, the fear that I had *only* unlocked it would creep up on me, forcing me to check again. I would spend the day at school spaced out and unable to focus on my work, thinking about the house, worried that I had ruined everything. At the time, I did not know that this is called obsessive-compulsive behavior, or that obsessive thoughts would be something I would struggle with on and off for the rest of my life.

Sometimes my compulsive thoughts would fade into the background. Sometimes they would come roaring back—especially during times of stress. Many years later, when I was an adult, a friend of mine came to visit. I was so ill that I couldn't eat. I could see the concern on her face as she watched me struggle to nibble on a cracker. "Try to remember that this is a feeling," she said, "and it will pass." Others had said similar things to me, but for some reason, that statement helped me realize that the problem was not that something terrible might happen. The problem was not the outer world at all. The problem was inside *me*, with my thoughts and feelings. Finally, my family was able to convince me to visit a psychiatrist.

And I did get better. It took time, and—even now, after years of cognitive behavioral therapy and medication—I still fall into obsessive thought patterns sometimes. But at least now I know what they are. They are uncomfortable, but I know that the discomfort will, eventually, pass away.

What I learned, through my journey, is that when someone is mentally ill, the ill person's thoughts and fears feel like *reality*. It doesn't occur to them that something is wrong with the way their brain is working. I didn't realize a doctor could help my fears go away. My ill mind was too busy trying to control the fear all by itself; I didn't see a way out until my friend assured me that there was one.

When Cole is kidnapped and trapped on the Nightmare Line—that's what OCD, anxiety, and depression are like. They suck away the *you*ness of you, leaving a shell person filled with fear and, often, anger. And it isn't always easy to help someone who is trapped like that. Really, the most important thing anyone can do, at first, is let them know that they *are* trapped. If the ill person can realize that, they have already taken the first step toward becoming free.

If you or someone you know is struggling with fear, or anger, or huge uncomfortable emotions, please let a trusted adult know. When someone's mind isn't working right, he or she needs to see a mental health professional. I want to tell you that just the way I found a way out, they can too.

There is a way out of the darkness, I promise.

Don't miss these books by
LISA PAPADEMETRIOU

Discover these stories of magic, friendship, and family.

HARPER
An Imprint of HarperCollinsPublishers

www.harpercollinschildrens.co